Namit Arora worked as a computer engineer before choosing a life of reading and writing. Raised in the Hindi Belt, he lived in Louisiana, Silicon Valley, Western Europe, and travelled through scores of countries before returning to India over two decades later. He is the author of *The Lottery of Birth: On Inherited Social Inequalities* (2017) and an upcoming book on travel and history. He won the 3QD Arts & Literature Prize in 2011. His web home is shunya.net.

Praise for *Love and Loathing in Silicon Valley*

'Namit Arora takes the lid off life in the Great Indian Dream of Silicon Valley.'—Jerry Pinto

'A moving and insightful portrayal of the immigrant's exile from authenticity. Written in the language of human relationships, Arora's novel will speak to anyone who's been a stranger in a strange land.'—Anil Menon, author of *The Beast with Nine Billion Feet*

'In his assured and sparkling prose, Namit Arora does for Silicon Valley what Tom Wolfe did for Wall Street in *The Bonfire of the Vanities*: with keen eye and sharp wit, he captures the culture and mores of the place [and] reveals what has gone so horrifically awry in America and what is still worth preserving.'—S. Abbas Raza, Founding Editor, 3 Quarks Daily

'A cleverly written tale with a social conscience featuring themes of family, inclusiveness, racial divides, and the theatrics of love.'—*Kirkus Reviews*

'Namit Arora writes with an enviable briskness and ease, and produces an engaging, incisive portrait of the Indian techie in Silicon Valley. [He] describes immigrant life with empathy but without pulling any punches.'—Suvir Kaul, A.M. Rosenthal Professor of English, University of Pennsylvania

'A fiercely honest and insightful story, with richly painted characters I could empathize with readily. The female characters are strong and the author gets into their minds in a way that is refreshing and illuminating.'—Cherry Mosteshar, author of *Unveiled: One Woman's Nightmare in Iran*

Love and Loathing in Silicon Valley

A Novel

NAMIT ARORA

SPEAKING TIGER

SPEAKING TIGER PUBLISHING PVT. LTD
4381/4, Ansari Road, Daryaganj
New Delhi 110002

First published in the US by Adelaide Books 2019
First published in the Indian subcontinent by Speaking Tiger 2019

ISBN: 978-93-89231-25-0
eISBN: 978-93-89231-26-7

10 9 8 7 6 5 4 3 2 1

Typeset in Sabon LT Std by SÜRYA, New Delhi
Printed at Chaman Enterprises, New Delhi

To India and America,
and the seven seas in between.

One

THIS IS NOT THE LIFE he wants, Ved thinks once again, exiting the airport in Palm Springs. His heart is not in it. None of his role models ever did this sort of work for a living. When he was nudged on this path in his teens—with its unspoken promise of a secure job, social status, and a fair and lovely wife—he had no idea it would turn out this way.

'Ved?' A broad-hipped event coordinator greets him with all the enthusiasm of a young poodle. 'Perfect, perfect. Good afternoon, I hope your trip was just great. It's wonderful to meet you. Welcome to Palm Springs. We're so excited you're joining us for the Omnicon Sales Conference.'

Ved wonders how some people manage to be so bright and breezy all day. He knows it is her job to make him feel like he has just flown into the most exciting experience anyone could imagine, but all he wants now is an evening of solitude in his hotel room. In the morning, he'll be thrust into a sales conference to kick off 2003 for Omnicon. It'll swarm with a thousand co-workers, drawn from the company's 60,000 employees in 130 countries.

'It's so exciting to have so many of you from around

the world,' she enthuses, leading him to a waiting minivan. 'We're excited, so very excited to hear all about, umm... what is it you're going to talk about?'

'A new line of network security products.'

'That's great! We've planned so many exciting things to fill your spare time, some great team-building activities,' she chirps. 'This is one of the biggest resorts here. Only the best for our geniuses. You'll have access to a golf course, a horse ranch, hot air balloons, or you can spend some me-time on the artificial lake. Do you like boats, Ved?'

'Yeah, I do.'

'You'll love the ones here,' she says. Approaching the resort, he is impressed by the starkness of the California desert around it. 'Though as a marketing manager at Omnicon you prolly don't get time for all that,' she rattles on. 'No wonder you're doing so well so young, and have risen up in your career...'

'No, not really,' he laughs, caressing the lapel of his grey jacket that he had picked up for $20 from a Goodwill Store. 'At 36, I'm well into late-middle age in Silicon Valley terms, and I've only reached employee grade nine on our corporate ladder, eight rungs below the CEO. That's with a recent promotion after three years at Omnicon.'

'Oh, you're too modest. I have no doubt your colleagues really appreciate your work.'

He shrugs. 'I'm actually quite dispensable. I just help our salespeople sell, with the right marketing tools and messages,' he explains, 'though I think I'm good at it, or at least good enough.' But she's already out of the minivan, doing her happy walk towards the hotel entrance.

§

The conference opens at 7:30 the next morning with a video recording of a high-energy rock band on four large screens. The band's screechy cacophony annoys Ved, but he is amused by the sight of his Japanese colleagues in dark suits clapping earnestly.

Ved finds a seat near the back. This too shall pass, he thinks, but then feels bad for being so out of it. In recent years, he has invested just enough in career development to survive without losing his pride. A software engineer by training, he began as a coder in Silicon Valley, but over time, unable and unwilling to compete with freshly-minted graduates, he has transitioned to his current role in marketing, which better utilizes his so-called soft skills.

The auditorium walls are covered in multicultural posters of pretty business people: shaking hands, smiling at computer screens, peering lovingly at Omnicon's boxy equipment—meant to convey the joy their products bring into this world. A gleaming red Ferrari stands outside the auditorium, awaiting the '2002 Salesman of the Year'.

'Every morning I wake up and think, what can I do for my customers today?' declares Omnicon's CEO, Greg Dyer, opening the proceedings. 'It's all about the passion within. That's what keeps my intense focus on the customer.' His body language and voice project authority and confidence. 'We're not just another tech company in the Valley. Our mission is to empower people, to build the human network of tomorrow.' His hour-long talk is laced with frequent references to excitement, power, speed, changing the world, and killing the competition.

'We need greater teamwork,' Greg adds. 'As that great American hero Dr. Martin Luther King said, "We may have all come on different ships, but we're in the same boat now."' Next to Ved, an older British colleague softly intones, 'Oh, puhleeze!' just as some people start clapping and others feel pressured to join in. Ved turns to him and smiles; there is hope yet.

Next comes a talk by a motivational speaker. Another huckster, presumes Ved. The speaker soon unveils his big idea: 'The true killer app is killing time.' He has written a book on it, *The Art of Killing Time*, included in all attendee bags. A quote on its cover proclaims it a *tour de force*. No way he's lugging this back home, thinks Ved. He discreetly leaves it on his chair and goes for lunch. Post-lunch sessions bring on 'death by PowerPoint' as new hardware, software, multimedia gadgets and gaming consoles are launched. Jargon fills the air: synergy, paradigm, bleeding edge, leverage, disruption, value-proposition, mission-critical, solution ecosystem.

§

In his room that night, Ved gets an email from Liz, confirming their very first date on Friday evening. A nervous flutter of excitement courses through him. If only he could fast-forward his week and get to Friday.

He 'met' Liz two weeks ago on a matchmaking website that came complete with expert advice, success stories, even tips on writing 'great emails'. Its pages featured handsome men and women, smiling, staring into each other's eyes.

It has been a while since Ved had a formal 'girlfriend'—four years to be precise, since Pooja. He longs to wake up to the softness and warmth of a woman's body, to languidly make love on foggy weekend mornings. What he seeks appears modest to him: a smart, open-minded woman of above-average beauty, independent means, pleasant disposition and a sexual appetite to match his own. He is not willing to settle for much less, at any rate not for long.

But signing up for a matchmaking service with a credit card smelled of desperation and defeat. This is not how he wants to find a lover. As he paid for the subscription, a mild wave of bitterness coursed through him. Where are the chance meetings and spontaneous combustion of the movies and literature, he wondered, where passions rise unbidden and sweep one away?

Why was he doing it then? What mysterious power compelled him? Another triumph of matter over mind? Avoid cynicism, he told himself, approach it with an open mind. What other options did he really have? Being an introvert, going out and chatting up single women felt unnatural, nor did his lifestyle give him the opportunities for doing so.

Still, in his fifteen years in the US, Ved has fallen in love with several women. He has had a few intense flings, especially in his twenties, mainly with women he met on his travels: a French teacher in Japan; a Canadian social worker in Holland; a Venezuelan architect in Guatemala. None lasted more than a few months. So bumbling and awkward those first encounters were too. He remembers all the headiness, the voluptuous agony and the ecstasy of discovering each new mind and body, the messy heartaches and breakups. He now thinks it was more infatuation than love—a young man's lust and yearning fused with clumsiness and inexperience.

He knows that even an ample combination of beauty and brains aren't enough. His temperament, values, and goals also need to align with his companion's—this is the hard part. Yet there is so much more: who can say what brings and keeps a man and woman together?

After signing up, he had written his own profile, which, he concedes, had an element of marketing spin, but he wrote it sincerely. It is not far from how he sees himself. It reads:

> Had we but world enough, and time
>
> At home both in India and the US, I am a liberal Indian man with a belief that the unexamined life is not worth living. I like to read. While I'm increasingly drawn to non-fiction, much of that too, I've found, is not immune from fantasy and tricks of the imagination.
>
> I've lived on three continents, speak four languages, and have traveled widely. Part of my identity is being an outsider, but I do not make much of this: so many around me are outsiders too. Often, I feel like an outsider in every nation.
>
> Reliance on inner resources and seeking clarity of thought and purpose are worthy goals to me. I also enjoy cooking, good food, wine, and sunshine. I tend to recoil from too much domesticity. I'm definitely easy-going, not in any rat race, but I do believe that if something is worth doing, it's worth doing well.
>
> I see a multiplicity of truths and values in the world and try to refrain from facile judgment. I'm often playful

> and spontaneous, and humor is an inescapable response when I look around. I prefer curious, thoughtful, free-spirited people who consciously try to understand others and to simplify their own lives.
>
> I grew up in north India, came to the US fifteen years ago for a post-graduate degree in computers and now work for a prominent multinational.

He found no good way to indicate his preference for good cooks. The idea of a lover baking for him or labouring over a multi-course dinner—and him reciprocating at other times or in other ways—is sensual to him; but he reckoned that saying so, especially as an Indian man, might send the wrong message. He attached a photo and checked the boxes indicating his atheism, his desire to not have children, and his preference for college-educated women within five years of his age. He browsed the profiles suggested by the matchmaking software and wrote to about twenty women, most of them white or Indian.

The only replies came from two Indian women. He was disappointed but not surprised. He believes that in terms of sex appeal, Indian men in America rate near the bottom of the pile. Most white women instinctively regard his ilk as socially conservative; sexist; gawky in speech, manner, and style; reeking of pungent curries; with oily hair, greasy skin, and a fatalistic devotion to pot-bellied idols. All in all, not so flattering.

The photo of the first Indian woman to respond suggested a calm and intelligent face, with a shapely body to boot. But she spelled badly, clobbered basic grammar, and used too many exclamation marks. When they spoke on the phone, he found her English accent distractingly unpolished. When she didn't call or write back, he was silently relieved.

The second was an attractive, Ivy League MBA, 32, on a fast-track career at eBay. After a few short emails, they met for dinner. At the very start of the evening, he fantasized about making love to her on his Moroccan carpet. She had had a love marriage in her early twenties before she came to America. She recounted the breakup, 'I don't know what I was thinking when we got hitched. He was sooo dull you cannot imagine!' She leaned forward and revealed with a snicker, 'The poor guy even got down on his knees and begged me to not leave.'

Her work was intense, she said, but her life was too plain and boring. She wanted adventure, excitement, weekend escapes and concerts. She wanted a balance between work and play. Soon, his interest in her started to flag, as did the conversation. She seemed to him poorly read, a workaholic, driven by fads, not curious enough. Nor did she seem the type to hop into bed without igniting the expectation of the whole marital enchilada. He sensed tantrums and theatre: more pain than gain. He stuck to polite conversation for the rest of the evening. No doubt she too had sensed a gap for she emailed a brief note the next day that effectively said: Thanks for meeting me, but we don't seem to be each other's type. Good luck with others.

Then just as he was losing hope, Liz replied. He immediately went online to reexamine her photo, a distant shot at a bus stop: a redhead, plainly dressed, a little plump, forty years old—four years his senior—a UC Berkeley graduate in literature. Her profile read:

> Seeking mind / body / soul connection
>
> I am caring, playful, passionate, a good listener, outgoing, and thoughtful. I enjoy hiking and walking, world music, and love to dance. Indeed, life would be dull without music and dance! I am an avid reader and love indie films and the performing arts. I consider myself spiritual but not religious and practice yoga regularly. Eastern thought enchants me. I was born in England and raised in Connecticut after my English parents moved to America.
>
> I make friends easily and I am generous and loyal to those close to me. In the past, I have liked socially conscious, liberal, and multicultural men. I melt before strong, original and confident types.
>
> I love international travel. I've also lived in England for four years. I work for a non-profit group, don't take myself too seriously (well, most of the time) and know it's important to laugh at myself. Write to me if you are honest, responsible, intelligent, communicative, reflective, affectionate, and not afraid of commitment or revealing your vulnerable side.

He recalled why he wrote to her in the first place. Though wary of the vulnerability clause and her enchantment with 'Eastern thought', he found the pros more compelling: she reads and travels and pays attention to non-Western cultures. Passionate too, that holds some promise. And she's indicated with a checkbox that she doesn't want children either.

He wrote back to her the same day and they exchanged a few rapid-fire emails. Last weekend, they spoke on the phone. She mentioned a French film she saw with a friend the previous night in San Francisco. 'I didn't like it much, though I generally prefer French films over Hollywood. This was a bit too self-absorbed for my taste.' After the film, she'd had dinner in the Tenderloin at Naan & Curry, which Ved also likes.

'I taught high school literature for eight years,' she told him. 'Loved introducing my students to non-white authors—Achebe, Rushdie, Mahfouz—but I had a hard time with some terribly disrespectful, disruptive, and even violent students.' The final straw was a gunfight that killed two of her students, after which she left to join an environmental NGO.

'I really want to visit India,' she said. 'I should tell you that my Grandpa was a British colonial officer in India. From his surviving letters, it's clear to me that he was a bloody racist, full of Churchillian disdain for you "wogs".' Her interest in India seemed genuine. She was articulate, had an appealing accent, a sonorous voice, and a pleasant laugh. They spoke for almost an hour. Near the end of the call, he asked her out.

§

A team-building event is scheduled for the final evening in Palm Springs. Ved dreads team-building events. They remind him of his place in the corporate machine: a puny gear that periodically needs lube and conditioning. He knows that in this system their collective output and efficiency matter above all else, but who needs juvenile games to rub this in? He dreads the small talk, the fake enthusiasm, the pretence of interest.

He considers calling in sick (diarrhea? vomiting? diarrhea plus vomiting?), but the evening is too pleasant to be holed up inside the room. Besides, he is curious about that part of the resort—the velvety green garden by the man-made lake. He will surely meet a few Europeans who find this American team-building stuff ridiculous too. So he goes.

Omnicon's contingent is soon divided into tribes of American Indians: Hopi, Navajo, Sioux, and others. They're to compete in quintessential 'Indian activities' like making a campfire, treasure hunting, pitching a nylon tent, and installing rope ladders. His tribe is Navajo, whose job is to build three campfires. It is just before sunset. The desert air is starting to cool.

The Navajos get a major boost when they discover a neat pile of ready-to-light prime firewood 200 feet away. Many Navajos, among them salesmen from Mexico, Dubai and China, display childlike enthusiasm in transferring the logs to brick-lined pits. What would real Navajos make of this? wonders Ved. Without sharing his tribesmen's elation or competitive zeal, he does his bit for the cause by tending a fire that burns evenly. The Navajos finish ahead of other tribes and are applauded by all. As other tribes finish, their members too congregate around the fires with beers, martinis, margaritas, and start bantering.

One of his fellow Navajos is Fardad, a field engineer from Los Angeles, who asks where Ved is from before revealing his own place of origin: 'Persia.'

'You mean Iran?'

'Yes,' Fardad says, then adds in a softer voice, unbuttoning his suede jacket, 'I think you'll understand. I say Persia because Iran has such bad PR in America:

Axis of Evil, fatwa-wielding mullahs, mandatory hijabs. Persia sounds neutral, even exotic, with its cats, rugs, and ancient culture. As it turns out,' he smiles, his chin shiny in the light, 'most Americans don't know that Persia is also Iran.'

A few metres away, Ved notices Greg expounding glibly to deferential regional sales managers trying to 'maximize face time' with the boss. It is good to be the King. Greg seems to have what one needs in a CEO today: bold ideas, hunger for success and growth, the cold and focused execution of a Navy SEAL. A serial entrepreneur, Greg is proud of recounting how he rapidly grew his last business—a hard drive company—from almost nothing to selling it for thirty billion dollars. Wall Street is unanimously in love with him and calls him, as one analyst put it, 'a visionary par excellence, a rock-star CEO'.

The din of conversation rises, dinner is served, and awards are given. Post-dinner recreation includes an ex-Olympian archer in a cowboy outfit shooting apples off his wife's head. Ved cringes with every shot, wondering if there are some things people won't do for a living. His colleagues, fuelled by alcohol, lustily applaud their daring performance. The evening ends with a dazzling display of fireworks befitting Omnicon's size and financial muscle.

Indeed, Ved thinks, what a vast enterprise Omnicon is! Even prominent government portfolios in most countries—say, the health ministry of Greece—lack the budget of an executive VP at Omnicon. Money is power and with it, corporations are changing the world, by hook or by crook. In a way, he too is on this leading edge of change. But what kind of change, he wonders. Oh, how he longs to know: Is the net impact of his daily labours good or bad for the world?

§

Ved returns on Thursday evening to his rental apartment at the edge of Noe Valley, San Francisco, on the second floor of an Art Deco style building that's at least sixty years old. In the four years he has lived here, he has explored the city's spaces and offerings—film festivals, art shows, plays, concerts, street fairs, even a course in conversational Spanish. Lately, his cultural forays have reduced, but he isn't ready to move south to cut his 50-minute commute to Omnicon in the heart of Silicon Valley. He still loves the idea of living in the city and is fond of its energy and rhythm, the surprise encounters it affords, its Mexican and Middle-Eastern eateries.

He spends part of the evening lounging on the bright Moroccan carpet in his sparsely furnished and tidy living room. The carpet is large enough for two lovers at play. It still amuses him to think that four years ago, in Marrakesh, he had chosen its dimensions with that goal in mind. Sadly, the carpet hasn't seen any action yet.

He retires to bed early, so he is amply rested for his big date with Liz tomorrow.

Two

THE FIRST THING HE NOTICES as Liz opens the door is that she is larger than she appeared in her online photo.

In the bright light of her living room, he takes in the pale round face that makes her lips look even thinner than they are, and a body that most people might put closer to 'full-figured'. All at once, even as he offers her the tulips, a wave of bitterness sweeps over him. She is far less attractive to him than he had imagined.

'Lovely flowers, thank you so much,' she says, not seeming to notice his crestfallen look. 'How was the drive?'

'Not bad,' he says, pulling himself together. 'Especially for Friday.' He silently berates himself. He should have asked her for additional photos, to avoid getting into this mess, but he did not; some principle about the beauty within held him back. Now he might as well relax and try to enjoy the evening. A voice in his head chides him for his pettiness. What if she too deemed him unattractive for his thinning hair, brown skin or hairy body?

'What a nice and cozy place!' he says, ignoring the smell of stale incense. Settling down on the sofa next to a console piano he asks with no great interest, 'Have you lived here long?' They are both visibly self-conscious.

'Four years, since I returned from England. Marin County reminds me of the English countryside. I like this apartment because it's "very seventies", though it's a bit rickety now—the floor creaks in places.'

He surveys the room. 'Is that your painting on the easel?'

'Yeah, my work-in-progress, inspired by a crumbling convent I saw in Honduras last year,' she says. She recently finished the one on the wall—a small black woman sitting on a park bench in a tropical garden, 'inspired by a recurrent dream of a lonely, middle-aged widow'.

'Wow! How long have you painted?' His interest in her perks up.

'Ten years or so. I'm not very good at it but it keeps me entertained, and paintings make great gifts for family and friends.'

He rises to study the one on the easel. 'You're too modest! This is very evocative. I like this far more than a lot I've seen in art museums: Kandinsky, Pollock, de Kooning, and the like.'

'Thanks! That's very kind. The trick is to get the critics to agree with you,' she says, 'and art collectors to pay the big bucks.'

'You know that saying about art critics? "No degree of mediocrity can safeguard a work against the determination of critics to find it interesting."' They laugh easily. Not a bad start, he thinks.

A black cat saunters in, jumps up on the couch next to her and climbs on her lap. 'Meet Kali, my loyal friend for nine years. She's the inquisitive kind and she loves to snuggle. Sadly, she now has diabetes.' Liz mentions daily insulin shots, periodic visits to the vet, a special diet. Ved has never had a pet and finds it touching that people can lavish such care on a chronically sick animal.

'What can I get you for a drink? Wine, cola, cranberry juice, water?' At least she is effusive, even has a pleasant smile, he thinks, starting to feel at ease. He asks for red wine, then gets up to browse her bookshelves: classics of Western literature, third-world magical realism, civil rights, feminism, psychology, yoga, New Age spirituality. On the coffee table is a book on Indian art with a dancing Shiva on the cover.

She returns with two glasses of wine, crackers and feta. 'How was your day at work?'

'Not too bad. Fridays are the best.'

'Do you like your job?'

He shrugs. 'It pays well for relatively easy work, so I've learned to put up with it. I mean, it was exciting for a few years after college, but then it began fizzling out. After all, how many careers chosen by people in their teenage years remain interesting for a lifetime?'

'That's true, but then why not do a job that's intellectually more nourishing?' she asks.

'I haven't been so lucky. I look for intellectual nourishment outside work.'

'Oh, that's sad, but do you feel your work is at least making a difference in the world?'

'Yes, I suppose it is making a difference by contributing to the cause of greater network security. I just can't get excited about this cause though,' he smirks.

'So why not do a job that's more meaningful to you?'

'I wish, but how many such jobs pay enough?'

'How much is enough?' she asks.

'Enough to be middle-class, to afford some of life's finer pleasures, like travel, eating out, taking breaks from work to pursue pet projects—to be able to buy time with money. Most jobs do not offer this. I sometimes wish I were a doctor, but it's too late for that.' A brief silence ensues. 'How about you, do you like your job? It's with a non-profit, right?'

'Yes, a non-profit environmental watchdog that rates common consumer products for their eco-friendliness, and I love working there. I have great coworkers—smart, funny, committed. I love our workshops, we actually educate people on using ecologically better alternatives and we can afford to be neutral because we use standard scientific tests, publish our methodology and results, and do not work for profit growth or shareholders.'

'Sounds very progressive. I recently read about an advocacy group that teaches people to consume less, only what they need, for instance—to not confuse wants with needs.'

She laughs, 'That sounds so un-American. Sadly, we avoid that aspect of education. We focus only on disseminating facts and creating awareness. It's amazing how little people know.' Kali saunters across the room and settles on her lap again.

'So does your job leave you enough time to enjoy the city?' he asks.

'Oh, I make time, especially to hang out with friends, watch a play or film, read, paint. The usual really. But tomorrow I'm planning to go for an anti-war rally in San Francisco.'

'Protesting the looming war in Iraq?'

She nods, 'Yes. We'll be calling out the warmongers. We'll also try to raise awareness about the rapidly rising discrimination against Arab-Americans.'

'Wow, you're the real deal: a street activist! Unlike me, an armchair complainer.'

She goes on to tell him how much she hates US foreign policy. 'Immoral,' she explains, as if to a child. 'What else can we expect in our glorious age of corporations and their hijacking of democracy?' Returning to the Middle-East she adds, 'If I were in charge, I would end all US aid to Israel and slap economic sanctions against it.'

'I would too, but let's continue this on our way out. Else we'll miss our dinner reservation,' he says, steering her out of the apartment.

§

The pizzeria is packed with people. A shapely young woman in a miniskirt leads them to a small corner table. Ved defers looking at her legs lest Liz notice this indiscretion.

They order a carafe of cabernet and a large vegetarian pizza with extra toppings. Like him, Liz is not only vegetarian but also into organic produce.

'When did you turn vegetarian?' she asks.

'Two years ago.'

'What prompted that?'

'I'm warning you, Liz. There are few things more tedious than a nouveau vegetarian expounding on his reasons for giving up meat.'

She laughs, 'Oh, I can handle that. Besides, it'll help me understand you better.'

'Well, I'm not a strict vegetarian. I just don't eat mammals.'

'See! That's interesting already. Why spare the mammals?'

'Because they're the closest to us. I can't say how much they think, but have you ever seen a lamb agitate before a butcher's machete? I did, in Egypt. It had backed up against the wall, terror in its eyes. It may well be mere instinct with no real awareness or mental trauma, but I now have my doubts. Without proof, what entitles me to assume the opposite—that other animals are mere automatons, a bundle of blind reflexes? If they are more than that and can anticipate or at least feel pain, then my meat-eating sponsors their suffering. Over time, as I saw more animals in the wild and in BBC documentaries, I began to see each species as wondrous and lovable in its own way—so full of its own animal being, keen to live and thrive—and the more barbaric seemed our raising and killing them for food, especially when we don't *need* to do so in order to survive.'

'Animals are lovable, sure, but why only spare the mammals?' She looks amused.

'Because I find it easier to empathize with them. They're social animals like us; many are even known to possess self-awareness. But I'm not stopping there, I'm moving down the chain. I rarely eat birds now, though it's proving hard to totally give up tandoori chicken. Next may be fish, even mollusks and insects.' His tone has turned playful.

'Oh, don't forget your reptiles!' she interjects, 'Or in your next life, you might be born as one.' Their laughter fails to rise above the Friday evening din at the restaurant.

'Interesting reasons,' she continues. 'Mine, I must admit, were more emotional at first. In my teens, I saw a documentary on US stockyards. The sight of animals packed in long rows of cages did it for me. I couldn't stomach their immobility, the sadness in their eyes. I began seeing their captive faces in the meat my mother served at home. This was long before I learned about the drugs and growth hormones they are given, or the unnatural corn-based diets, even meat and bone meal, that are fed to vegetarian farm animals.

'I'm now thinking about turning vegan. I'm convinced that to rely on any animal product is to consign that species to manipulative breeding, hormones, drugs, and other horrible stuff to maximize yields and profits. The only way to break this cycle of cruelty and exploitation is to not rely on animals for any product, food or otherwise, if we don't have to.'

'Yes, well said. I relate to your reasons too.' A birthday song, sung by the restaurant staff for a patron, distracts them. Ved is quietly amused by the phoniness of the spectacle.

'So have you met any interesting people through online dating?' she asks.

'Not really. Many of the women I wrote to seemed interesting, but I guess they were not looking for my type.'

'Well, most interesting men aren't looking for my type either. One man asked me for additional photos, which I sent. He promptly wrote back that he was looking for something different. His loss, I consoled myself. At least he was honest.'

Ved squirms in his chair and averts his eyes. Liz continues, 'But I've dated a few. The last guy was Mehdi, an Egyptian-American doctor, and before him an Iranian and an Italian. None lasted more than a few months. They were all so flaky, so afraid of commitment. A friend recently advised me to try what she called "my own kind" again—a white American that is.'

'Advice you don't appear to have taken, if I am any clue.'

'I thought about it, but I find them a little too boring,' she chuckles.

'Why?'

'I'm not too fond of this culture and its legendary insularity, and white American men are its products. There are exceptions, but American men seem so devoid of soul. Too focussed on getting and achieving. I find them too linear, plastic, bland, if you know what I mean. In fact, I tend to get along better with white Europeans.'

'So, when was your last major relationship?'

'It ended four years ago,' she replies, her voice growing sombre. 'An English guy, Peter. We were together for seven years. We had our differences—he didn't care for art or travel, for instance; he mostly read pulp fiction and business books—but our politics and sense of humour were similar. I grew close to his family; his sisters and I became good friends.'

Pausing for a second as if recalling a painful memory, she explains that things began going south after he landed an audio equipment franchise. It made him good money, more than he ever had before. Slowly but surely, he became a workaholic and they started drifting apart.

At first, they fought over mundane matters: home decor, money, weekend plans. Then he began criticizing her taste in art, once even in front of their friends. At one party, she screamed at him so he fumed and sulked for weeks. Their respect for each other hit new lows. She expected things to get worse, but nothing prepared her for the bomb he dropped one day: he was leaving her for someone he had met three months earlier, a 'bloody customer' of his.

'It took me the better part of two years to get over it.'

'Are they still together?'

'I'm not sure. They moved to Florida last year. I met her at a party once. She really is as dumb as a doormat. I still don't know what he sees in her except that she is the sort of young, skinny blonde that men like to chase. Can you imagine doing something like that?'

A rhetorical question but he chimes in, 'Unlikely. I consider the brain a must-have.'

'All men say that, until the next clueless skinny blonde comes along,' she says half-jokingly, half-cynically.

'It's not as simple as beauty or the brain,' he says. 'Like most people, I think I need a bit of both—even for a fling. What's more important to me is whether or not she has the fear of the darkie in her, whether the possibility of having sex with my kind gives her the creeps. A woman with this fear is *ipso facto* not attractive to me, whatever the world might think of her.'

'Wow,' she responds with a start, 'that's interesting, and so true. It has to be a huge factor on matchmaking sites, as in who people write or respond to.'

'I think so,' he says solemnly, 'the fear of the darkie,

I think, lurks within too many people and it takes an enormous conscious effort, of education and experience, to be rid of it. Indians have it too, for people darker than themselves, especially African-Americans.'

'I agree. There is still so much prejudice out there,' she echoes his solemn tone, takes a sip of wine. 'It's really sad. Sometimes I lose all hope for humanity.'

Unlikely, he thinks, that she understands this shade of prejudice and its distinctive sting from within. Nothing unusual in that. There are lots of prejudices in the world whose sting he too has never known from within.

'How about you?' she asks, 'when did your last relationship end?'

Does his relationship with Sasha count? It is a kind of relationship. No, he reckons, she means a relationship with long-term romantic interest, or at least its possibility. 'The last significant one ended four years ago. She was an Indian-American woman, Pooja.'

'What went wrong?'

'We got off to a good start, but we wanted different things from life. I mostly wanted long-term companionship, she wanted more—a family with kids.'

'That's hard. It's best to agree about such things at the beginning.'

'We did! We had made a mutual pact to not have children. However, two years into it, just when we had started living together, she changed her mind, and we had a huge fight.'

'I know another couple who went through this. So you two just parted ways?'

'If only,' he sighs. 'Pooja changed her mind *after* she

got pregnant by accident. The condom broke. We fought bitterly the evening her test came out positive. When I suggested abortion, she told me to go to hell. It was her baby, her body, her decision. I had done my bit. If I didn't want to be involved, she would skip naming the father in all official documents. She said she had the means to raise the child by herself. I was so upset that when she refused to budge, I moved out of our apartment three days later. We had been living together for five–six months.'

'You broke up over that?'

'It wasn't like everything else was great between us. Living with her was harder than I had expected. We had begun to fight over trivial things, and that drained me. It strained our relationship to the point where I had talked about breaking up. Three months after our eventual breakup, she moved to Houston where she grew up, and now lives with her mother and sister.'

'She had the baby, then?'

'Yes. A girl, now three or so, but I've never seen her. This may sound terrible, but I didn't want to. She is not my child, and meeting her would have its own complications.'

'Huh, what do you mean not your child?'

'I didn't bring her into this world, Pooja did. I was only a sperm donor. It's not sperm that makes a child, or a father. Intention and love do. She's her child, not mine.'

They are quiet for a while as the waitress brings the pizza and serves them a slice each.

'That's a pretty hard line to take, but I can also understand it,' she says.

'I'm glad. Few of my friends can. I lost some friends over this.'

'They probably saw your decision as too cold and heartless.'

'Yeah. I think they fetishize parenthood and saw my approach as "unnatural." Never mind that I hadn't wronged anyone here, nor broken any obligations or promises.' He adds after a pause, 'Still, it's not like I'm completely at peace with the situation, though only I know that every other alternative would've been much worse for me.'

'Why were you so adamant about not having children?'

'I like children, it's not that, but I've never, even for a minute, longed to be a father myself. Really. Whenever I've considered the possibility, I've found it unpalatable. I guess I just don't have the fatherhood gene that most men seem to have. Besides, I thought, wouldn't children raise my stakes in the world, reduce my mobility and freedom? Wouldn't I need to hunker down, compromise more for their sake, live more fearfully? Kids are so vulnerable, so impressionable. I would agonize over them endlessly—their values, health, education. I too might turn into a freak obsessing over things like safe pedestrian crossings near their school, playground surfaces, and other everyday life experiences. Can one avoid doing so and still be a good parent? Indeed, how would I raise a child, given how outmoded I often feel, out of step with the world? It would be hard to see them fumble through life, as I did—still do. Why bring this upon myself and upon them? I saw no good reasons.' He pauses for a sip of wine.

'I mean,' he continues, 'I look around at my friends and it's not appealing at all—sure, children bring a kind of joy in their lives, but they also fuel a lot more self-absorption, shrunken horizons, and mundane battles of will and power over food, values, homework, piano lessons, science fairs. Given their parenting and milieu, the children will likely grow up into competitive little twits devoid of soul. Remember that Larkin poem?—"They fuck you up, your mum and dad / They may not mean to, but they do..."

'Ha, yes. A classic.'

'Indians of course fuck up their kids in their own ways,' he adds. 'No, that life is not for me, I decided long ago—I'd live a different life, cultivate greater self-awareness, and be free.'

'Be free?' She pauses to chomp a piece of blackened zucchini, 'Peter used to say that too, it was apparently why he was against marriage. Until, of course, he met that *chica*. What exactly do you want to do with your freedom?'

'Well, it's an end in itself, a state of mind. It makes more things possible. Life is so horribly short anyway. We barely have time enough to learn something about our place in the world, to come to terms with death, and to prepare for it with a calm and lucid dignity.'

'Ooh,' her eyes widen, 'that's rather morbid. But think of the joy and levity children bring too. Aren't you missing out on an experience that's so central to being human?'

'Well, children bring suffering too, especially if they turn out to be like Dubya or Dick Cheney.' They both laugh. 'But yes, if I forego that joy, I also free myself up for other joys and experiences that are also central to being human. You win some, you lose some.'

'You make it sound so simple. The urge to procreate is a fundamental human instinct. There is something so primal about it,' she says, looking serious.

'Well, not all of us have it in equal measure. Moreover, it's an instinct we share with other animals. Why dignify or embrace all of our instincts? What's so noble about procreation? It's the easiest thing to do. Countless people do it every day. In fact, by using other human gifts—our consciousness, language, reason, wonder—don't we often try to tame many of the instincts we share with other animals? For Toynbee, that's the whole meaning of civilization.'

'Fair enough, but sometimes I feel we've all become super selfish—who needs children, we say, let's just live for ourselves. We've become good at justifying our selfishness.'

'Umm, I disagree. I think those who procreate are no less selfish. They do it entirely for themselves! They certainly don't do anybody else any favours, certainly not those yet unborn—'

'That's too simple,' she interrupts. 'I think there is also a spiritual dimension to the so-called miracle of childbirth, and in raising children. It's part of what makes us human. There are times when I think the one big mistake of my life was not getting pregnant at sixteen in the back seat of a car,' she chuckles and then turns serious. 'My child would've been an adult by now. In some ways, it would have made me a better person I think—more giving, connected, rooted.'

Ved thinks how, by contrast, he considers himself a small winner for having prevailed over all forces pushing him to procreate. 'But now I'm confused,' he says. 'In your profile, didn't you indicate that you are not interested in having children?'

'I did, but the honest truth is that I never found a man who wanted children with me, and now, well, I think I'm too old. It's not like I see this only as a loss—not at all. Look at where the world is heading. A bleak future awaits our young. Everywhere you look, things like caring, spirituality, and basic human decency and trust are being squeezed out by competition, greed, a winner-take-all ethic. It's so disturbing. Life has become such a race, a stupid fucking contest!'

The waitress brings the bill. 'I'll get it,' he declares, picking it up instinctively.

'No, let's go Dutch,' she protests.

'You can get it the next time,' he says awkwardly, trying to come across as neither a cheapskate, nor a chauvinist. Dividing it evenly didn't seem fair to him either; after all, the amount on the bill mattered much less to him than to her.

The air outside is crisp. They walk to the car and drive back to her place.

'Thanks, Ved, I had a great time,' she says, as he turns into her street.

'Likewise, Liz. Time just flew by,' he says and returns her smile.

They step out of the car. He only manages a quick, clumsy hug before they turn away.

Driving home, he reflects on the evening. No, he felt no great sparks between them. Yet, while she is no beauty, she is rather intelligent. A good listener too. And wasn't he comfortable in her presence, able to talk about so much after so long? That's surely worth something. All in all, he decides that he wouldn't mind another date to see where it leads.

Three

On Saturday afternoon the next day, Sasha calls to ask, 'Are you free?'

Sasha is a Russian escort, twenty-eight, slim, dark-haired, with green eyes. 'Hey, can you give me a ride in an hour to the Plaza Hotel please? I have had a wonderful break, three days to myself, but now I pay. I have a job, two hours, but my stupid car—it won't start. I'll make up to you,' she coos at him.

Ved imagines her pacing in the living room in her red silk robe. He can practically smell her perfume on the phone. 'I'll pick you up in fifty minutes. Be ready and wait downstairs.'

§

He found her almost a year ago on a website advertising escort girls. Fragments of her ad have stayed with him: 'I am all natural, very fit...I specialize in fantasy role-plays: nurse, housemaid, nun, schoolgirl (special requests welcome)...My Russian accent will make you putty in my hands, in all seven languages I speak.' She had posted several revealing photos.

They first met last summer at the Plaza Hotel. It had been over a year since he got laid, a deprivation that had made even his daily encounters with women unduly sexualized. At times, even casual physical contact with a woman—say, an accidental hallway collision at work, or the customary greeting hug—made him tingle with a sense of illicit delight.

After much uneasy deliberation, he had called her for a two-hour tryst. On a whim, as he was leaving the house to meet her, he picked up a porcelain figurine of a dancing Ganesha that a friend had given him. The hotel lobby teemed with a tour group from East Asia. No one noticed his nerves as he made his way to her room.

'For you,' he gave her the Ganesha, 'he'll remove all obstacles in your path.'

She was greatly amused. 'That's my kind of god, a dancing one too,' she gushed, and mimicked his dancing pose. 'Thank you!' She glowed in her pink chiffon dress. Her youthful voice and accent instantly charmed him.

They sat close to each other on the couch. He settled the charges upfront: $400.

Raised in St. Petersburg, she had come to the US eighteen months earlier. 'I am not illegal person,' she said, which sounded strange. 'I have permit to stay, but not to work.'

So she resorted to this secret work. Until a year earlier, before becoming an escort, she was an exotic dancer in a club. Her roommate, a Ukrainian woman, introduced her to both jobs.

'So what do you like to do in your free time, Sasha?'

'Read books, watch TV,' she said. She had a sweet smile, pearly white teeth, and high cheekbones. 'I like Pushkin and Gogol. Ah, you know them? I also read mystery novels. I don't like American TV, so stupid you know, I only like PBS and Discovery channels.'

'Very nice,' he said, letting his imagination roam her curves, her smooth burnished skin. 'Your English is very good.' The conversational foreplay felt decadent, delicious, for he knew it would happen. It was just a matter of minutes. Putty in her hands, huh.

'I've never been with an Indian man,' she said. Inching closer, she brushed a finger on his chin, traced it down his arm, lifted his hand, and pressed it to her bosom. Well-practiced, then, a professional. He leaned over, nuzzled his nose on her slender neck. She smelled nice. At the barest of hints, she sidled into an embrace. He let his fingers wade through her long black hair, down her shoulder, over her breast beneath her pink chiffon dress.

They moved to the bedroom. He undressed when she went to the bathroom. She emerged to find him tucked beneath the soft white sheets. She slipped off her dress as he watched, hopped into bed, and fell into his embrace. She was pliant, eager to please, and skilled at touching a man. He groped; his thirst for her body astounded him. They did it missionary style. She grunted at his frantic thrusts, responding with joyous abandon—feigned, no doubt—but loud enough to make him imagine otherwise. When it was over, he promptly rolled off to her right, exhausted.

As the mental fog lifted, he reflected on their coupling. Man: half reason, half appetite. How ridiculous, to be held hostage by a silly appendage between his legs. Humiliating, in fact.

They lay together with her head on his chest, a

pseudo-intimate moment. He caressed her neck and back. 'I like your touch,' she said, 'you are good lover. I think you are good man too.'

'How many others do you say this to?' he laughed.

'You don't believe?' she asked. 'I think eyes are windows to the soul. I see kindness in your eyes, and sadness too. Is there something troubling to your heart?'

She adores the idea of being an artist, she said that evening. 'I want to make sculpture, pottery. I learned in Russia. I am very passionate person, as all true artists should be.' Artists, he thought, are now everywhere—body artists, computer artists, porn artists—and wondered about her notion of art. 'I love Indian music,' she revealed, 'flute and sitar music.'

'Why not get wife from India?' she asked teasingly. 'No more loneliness.'

'I have never considered that option,' he said. 'Now it's too late. All the good women, as my mother says, are taken. Not even Ganesha can help.' This made her laugh.

She receives many, what she calls 'funny offers' of marriage from lonely white men, but she eventually hopes to find true love, marriage, children, a normal family life. Prior to this work, she had slept with only two men, both boyfriends. Now she services two or three men daily, on occasion in threesomes with her roommate. 'I have many boyfriends now,' she smiled. It is part of her job, to put up pleasant faces: service with a smile, the secret of customer loyalty.

Her phone rang as he was getting dressed. She stepped into the bathroom to take the call. He heard her giving directions. Another client was due in an hour. Time enough to make the bed, air the room, wash herself clean of him, and slip on that pink chiffon dress again.

§

He finds her waiting at the curbside outside her apartment. She is wearing high heels, sheer stockings, a turquoise dress revealing her Wonderbra cleavage, and a matching purse with the usual tools of her trade: lotions, sprays, condoms, lubricants, hairbrush, mints, cellphone.

She climbs in and leans over for a friendly kiss. 'How are you?'

'I'm fine.' He surveys her form, 'Beautiful dress!'

'Thanks,' she looks pleased. 'Long time no see. Many weeks.'

'I've been travelling on business,' he lies.

'Is there another woman? A girlfriend?'

'I was busy with work, a new product launch.'

'Did you miss me?' She reaches out and rubs his crotch with her hand.

'My whole mind and body misses your whole mind and body,' he smiles.

'Liar,' she withdraws her hand. 'My roommate fell and fractured her leg, and for the last three days I've been taking care of her. Great time for my car to break down today.'

'How is work these days?' he asks.

'Not as good as before, because the stock market has fallen, no? My clients talk about it. One man said his company went into Chapter 11, which happens when there is no money left.'

'I know. It might get worse.' When they reach the Plaza Hotel he says, 'Call me when you are done.'

Who would've thought, thinks Ved, that he would someday chauffeur a prostitute friend to work? He parks, finds a cafe, and browses *The Chronicle*. The Pope has proclaimed another saint and beatified three others. He has made more saints than his predecessors in the last four centuries combined. Ironic, Ved thinks, that it should happen in such unsaintly times.

Suddenly a procession appears a block away. Hundreds are marching, shouting slogans, raising placards: Peace Now; Justice for All; Who Would Jesus Bomb?

People step out of local businesses and cheer loudly. Cops are in tow to prevent possible unrest; traffic is being diverted. He has never joined a protest march and suddenly longs to do so, at least for a few blocks. Then he recalls, this might be the anti-war rally Liz planned to attend. If they met, what reason would he give for being here? What if she offered to hang out with him after the rally? So he stays in the cafe. He strains his neck against the window but does not spot her in the crowd.

§

After their first encounter, Ved had again hired Sasha twice in just one month, both times at his place. Both times he spent the rest of the evening in bed, savouring the smell of sex and her perfume in the sheets. They clicked in many ways: sexual chemistry, temperament, being cultural outsiders. Clicked to the extent of making their encounters simple and pleasurable to him, but he knew he couldn't afford her this often. Soon this would have to stop.

He reflected on the balance of power between them—

say, between his power of money versus her power of beauty. If it weren't for him, he reckoned, there would be another man. At least she is safe with him. If he is using her, she too is using him. Is symbiosis immoral? Alas, if only the morality of all this could be as plain as the cost-benefit metrics he creates for Omnicon's products.

From what he could tell, she liked him too and opened up to him. She shared details about her family. 'My father loved Raj Kapoor films,' she said.

A pharmacist in the Soviet era, he now lives a retired life in St Petersburg. Her mother, a schoolteacher, died six years ago. As a child, Sasha wanted to become a ballerina, but her training stopped when her father left the family to be with another woman.

She revealed this without bitterness. 'I'm not very close to my father, but I've been thinking of him lately and want to see him before he dies.'

She mentioned her desire for a child, to deeply experience the mother-child bond that she thinks is 'above all others in the world'. Towards the end of their third session, she said, 'You already know more about me and my thoughts than any other man in America.'

On her next visit, to his great surprise, she insisted on waiving her fee. He fought the idea but she dismissed it. 'I think you'll stop seeing me otherwise. You are smart, with open mind, and treat me well. We can be friends. I make enough. Just give me flowers when we meet.'

He was delighted, but also worried. The clarity of their contract was lost. Who would call the shots now? He struggled to understand her motivations. Was she playing a mean game?

They began meeting about twice a month. He has cooked for her twice and taught her to make dal and baingan bharta. They've seen *The Gangs of New York* in a theatre, eaten at Naan & Curry, and smoked pot twice. However, more often than not, she would be the one to decide when they met, usually on short notice. On some visits, there would be no sex. He noted with mild chagrin that over time, more of her visits began happening during her off days from work: her periods. All told, they'd had sex around a dozen times.

Mindful of her loss of income with him, he once took her shopping to a store on Union Square. She picked out two dresses, lingerie, and a pearl and emerald necklace.

One Saturday, on a whim, he had taken her to the Museum of Modern Art. She saw it with rapt attention. As they left the museum, she said, 'Art really is like beauty. It depends so much on the eye of the observer.' He asked about the art she liked, from which he deduced that her aesthetic leaned towards moody portraits and landscapes, organic shapes and earthy colours. They liked many of the same pieces.

One weekend he showed her some of his travel pictures. She loved the ones from the Galapagos Islands and asked if he would help her plan a trip there. He said yes, but it turned out to be a fleeting thought. He showed her pictures of Agra, his hometown in India. He gives her credit for never asking why they worshipped cows in his country.

She has told him about some of her clients. How weird, she once said, that so many businessmen want office sex—on office desks or chairs, one wanted it on the boardroom table, another atop a copier. With a laugh, she recalled a man who simply asked to be tied to a leash and pulled around his house on all fours. She once complained of a tingling butt—she had let a client pursue a spanking fantasy and it had gone a little too far.

He has been to her apartment once and met her roommate, Olga, who has recently shot her first adult flick, something Sasha considers beyond the pale for herself. That evening, as they ate Chinese take-out, he fantasized about a threesome but has never pursued it. Once while Olga was away, Sasha invited him over. She made a beef steak dinner for him with such attention and joy that he just couldn't tell her he doesn't eat mammals, and even pretended to enjoy it. She later got playful in bed and showed him some tricks with her vaginal muscles.

He likes that his relationship with Sasha has minimal expectations. He finds her curious about the world and pleasant to be with. He is glad to have her disrupt his loneliness, but he is also happy to return to his solitude after she leaves. She's at most a 'friend with benefits', or, as some might put it, a 'fuck buddy'. He would likely resent her if she began demanding more from him, though the reverse seems to him true as well.

He still wonders about her motivations: what does she get from him? Perhaps she too is lonely and is willing to trade sex for the companionship he provides, such as it is. Indeed, he thinks, if she can routinely trade sex for money, why not trade sex for agreeable company?

§

Two hours later, he watches her amble back to the car, newly fucked, pawed, squeezed by a man now perhaps sprawled across his king-sized hotel bed, satiated. Her hair is in relative disarray. 'Welcome back. Everything okay?'

'Yes, fine,' she gets into the car. Her client was a white man around Ved's age, an East Coast sales rep for a pharma company, visiting headquarters. 'He comes here every month. He gave me this silver bracelet today,' she raises her wrist, smiles.

'Nice. Did he also ask you to marry him?'

'Very funny.' She pinches his arm and asks, 'What now? Shall we go to your place?'

'I would love to, but I have a friend visiting from out-of-town this evening,' he lies. Truth is that he wants to keep her on the back-burner until he knows how things turn out with Liz.

'I'll call you,' he says. They make small talk until he drops her outside her place.

§

Brushing his teeth before bed, the pain in his molar returns again. It is one of his rare sporadic ailments. To stay healthy and fit, he visits a gym three–four times a week and pays attention to his diet. He is still handsome by Indian standards but feels past his prime. The indignity of aging awaits him too. What will his decay and old age look like? He imagines a bent back, achy joints, hearing aids; he imagines disposable diapers after losing control of his bowels, his caretaker's disgust at his shit-smeared bottom. Add dementia and life might again revolve around eating, sleeping, and defecating unpredictably—exactly what befell his grandfather. And what of his implacable sexual appetite? Will it fade in old age? He hopes it does. The world does not take kindly to horny old men.

He often thinks about death. Not in a morbid way but as a simple fact of life that informs his choices and opinions. When the hour comes, he hopes to approach it with a fearless calm. But he must first write a living will, designate beneficiaries for his possessions. It should clearly say: In case of terminal unconsciousness, take me off life-support; donate all usable body parts.

Shortly before sleeping, his laptop 'dings'. He notices an email from Liz.

> Dear Ved,
>
> Hope your weekend is going well. Let me say again that I really enjoyed meeting you and would love to see you again (I haven't heard from you. I hope this feeling is mutual).
>
> I want to clarify something upfront. In speaking of your ex, you said you only wanted companionship, while she wanted more. Shall I be frank? For me, marriage, per se, is not required, but monogamous commitment is, along with a consistency of presence, and a willingness to invest in each other through time, consideration, thought, and action. I'm not looking for someone to only hang out with from time to time, but a partner in life. Are you open to this possibility?
>
> I have landed two tickets to the San Francisco Ballet (free!) from a friend who has season tickets and cannot attend. If you're still interested, would you like to join me for a show next Saturday? It's an old Balanchine and will be prettier than the modern ones tend to be.
>
> Kali says hello. Liz.

He replies promptly.

Dear Liz,

The feeling is mutual indeed. I meant to write but was out most of the day.

Thanks for being frank. I quite prefer it myself. To your point, all I can say is that, in general, I'm not averse to the idea of commitment or a partner in life. In other words, I am willing to give it an honest try and see where it leads.

I would be delighted to see the ballet with you. This would be my first live performance! Dinner afterwards?

Bye for now. Ved.

Four

Monday morning at work, Ved walks past Omnicon's new poster art in the corridors: a lone bald eagle in flight, muscular rowers in a longboat, lean multicultural climbers scaling snowy peaks. Each has a hokey inspirational message below. There's also art that was once anti-establishment but has long been defanged and made chic: a Diego Rivera mural; a wall-sized woodcarving of Ché Guevara's shaggy face—presumably to inspire 'the rebels' in their ranks, rebels, who like him, work in identical beige cubicles in a large carpeted hall to raise Omnicon's profits.

In his first meeting, he endures a visiting British colleague who spouts jargon with possessed élan. He speaks fast: 'My charter is risk management, knowledge extension, empowering feet on the street...competition is intense...we are in daily dogfights...the European theatre needs better products faster.' His body language is aggressive, he is clearly used to dominating conversations. Ved is mildly repelled by the man.

In his second meeting, a woman from Operations addresses a group of marketers about proactive cost management. Ved's eyes roam her curvy body. In a reverie, he imagines her naked on his Moroccan carpet, legs spread, yielding to his touch. Might this serious, bookish transplant from Middle America turn into a hot little siren in bed? Snapping out of his daydream, he chides himself. It has again been too long since he got laid, he thinks. So ridiculous, his wayward libido, always making an ass of him. Good thing he can often laugh at it too.

Ved has lunch at his desk. He prefers the quiet of his office to the desultory cafeteria talk on weather, weekend plans, blockbuster movies, the stock market, office politics, and the like. Nothing more personal or substantial is ever discussed, such as sex, death, religion, literature, or geopolitics. In a competitive arena that hires people based on narrow skills, revealing more about oneself risked exposing one's vulnerabilities too. To be professional is to be discreet and formal, to operate from behind a mask. So the private lives and beliefs of even the colleagues he interacts with daily are opaque to him. Who knows what secrets lurk within the hearts of his co-workers? Of course, sometimes it is better not to know.

Many times each day, he detaches himself from the present. Watching from above, so to speak, he sees the panorama of his theatre: Has blind evolution really led to all this, *all this,* in the deafening silence of the cosmos? So ephemeral, yet we live as if we were eternal: consumed with trivialities, infatuated with false gods and vain totems of power—none too different from the ancient Egyptians labouring to raise an obelisk. At times, this unsparing view of life provokes a quiet, brooding sorrow. How beautiful, he thinks nevertheless, this theatre-watching ability.

§

For Friday lunch, Ved meets Ravi, a younger colleague who came to the US some years ago via an IT consulting firm in Bangalore and later joined Omnicon. Ved sees him as a circumstantial comrade. 'You look unhappy,' Ved observes. 'Is everything okay?'

'I'm just pissed off at Angie, that Marcom babe. This morning she accused me of not following company guidelines for tradeshow giveaways. What a fuckin' control freak!'

'Business as usual then. I was half-hoping for some juicy stories.'

Unlike most Indian men in Ved's orbit, Ravi is not shy about discussing his love life—or lack thereof—with his friends.

'Man, that's not funny,' Ravi smiles, revealing his professionally whitened teeth. 'I'm still hurting from the last one.' He means the Fijian sales admin he managed to get into bed some months ago. The affair ended badly and she recently left Omnicon. This came after failed attempts at courting two other women colleagues the previous year.

'Given my luck,' Ravi continues, 'I might have to settle for the India solution. I want to sleep with an American chick before that though.' He means a 'white chick', a conquest, not someone to marry. Ravi has by now tried everything—bars, hobby clubs, singles events, online dating, golf, language courses—all without success. When Ved once suggested the hooker route, Ravi's response was surprisingly prudish. 'I'm not ready to stoop that low, dude,' he said.

'All I need is to get laid once in a while, man,' Ravi

goes on, 'That's all I really need from women.' His eyes track a young redhead across the cafeteria and he strokes his slick black hair like a yesteryear Bollywood villain. 'Oye, Basanti,' he whispers and chuckles impishly.

Don't waste your time on her. You are invisible to her, Ved wants to say but does not. 'Tell me about the India solution. Is it more than a passing thought this time?'

Ravi nods, then turns sombre. 'I'm thirty, man. I'm tired of being alone. It's not just sex—that's only the minimum need. I also want someone to come home to. Loneliness is killing me, man. I fuckin' end up drinking most evenings.'

Ved knows Ravi is more than half-serious. Ved tries to imagine him with a fresh-off-the-boat Indian woman. 'What would be your criteria?'

'It's pretty simple, yaar, a modern, cosmopolitan babe from a metro, mid-twenties, not too conservative. The less into that puja-shuja business the better. Educated enough to get a job here, mild-mannered, healthy, and of course, a decent cook.'

'Hard to beat hot aloo parathas and lassi for breakfast, aye,' Ved's tone is playful. 'For the range of services you want, what you're really looking for is an Indian geisha.'

'On the job training, man,' Ravi laughs. 'One can always teach a new dog old tricks.'

Ravi's parents have probably begun a search already, thinks Ved. He imagines Ravi's matrimonial ad in the Delhi edition of the *Times of India*:

> Seeking tall, fair, slim, beautiful, convent-educated career girl, 24–29, for our handsome Punjabi Khatri son, fair, 30, 5'10", San Francisco, USA job, H1-B visa. Six-figure

dollar salary. Reply with girl's bio-data and full-length pictures.

'Here, have some freedom fries,' Ved offers with a laugh. As Ravi extends his hand to grab a few, Ved notices a shiny new Rolex on his hand. 'Wow, you bought that?'

'Looks real, right?' he replied with a grin that can appear only on the face of a desi who believes he has struck an unbelievable bargain. 'Indistinguishable,' he declares. Last year he had bought this replica on a whim for $17 from a chor bazaar in Hong Kong.

The conversation drifts to stocks. Ravi's bullish plays have failed him—the NASDAQ has tumbled in the last eighteen months of the dotcom crash, starting almost right after he bought a sporty BMW. 'What the fuck, yaar,' he mutters in bafflement. 'Why is it imploding like this?' Most of his stocks are now worth pennies on the dollar. Ved's own bets have fared no better but at least he hadn't expanded his lifestyle based on paper net worth.

'Think of the bright side,' Ved tries to console, 'It's character building.'

'It must be, because all this green character stuff is oozing out of my ears and dribbling down my chin. I'll happily swap some of it for cold hard cash,' he laughs.

'Funny! Didn't you recently go on a business trip to Hawaii? How did you manage that?'

He guffaws, 'I'm a smooth operator, man. I recycled an old white paper for the Connecting People Conference, then lobbied to get past Omnicon's restrictions on business travel by citing our rival's presence there.'

'So how did it go?'

'The gods were kind. My 30-minute gig was on the first morning after which I bailed out of the three-day conference. I was on the Big Island with a convertible—Avis loves me and gave me a free upgrade. I bummed around in perfect weather, snorkelling, having margaritas and tiger prawns on the beach, but the highlight was definitely the lava flows at the volcano.'

'You lucky dog!'

§

After lunch, Ved meets Roger, his manager, for a weekly update. He sees Roger as a shrewd and pragmatic man who, unlike himself, takes a keen interest in company politics and is a charming extrovert. A self-avowed 'Euro-mutt', Roger once claimed that his paternal ancestry—'the scum of Irish society'—even includes a convicted horse thief. He is pale and stocky, with a receding hairline, a thick brown moustache, blue eyes, and a loud infectious laugh.

Roger says he believes in personal responsibility, minimal gun control (he owns three guns), and a strong national defense. The liberal tones of National Public Radio send his blood pressure soaring. When he became Ved's manager last year, he told Ved, 'I like to work hard and play hard.' With Roger, the equation seems simple: make me look good and I'll look out for you. He describes his management style as hands-off, which it indeed is. On many days, they don't make contact at all. Ved largely manages his own time, an aspect of his job he loves.

A few cubicles down from Ved is a web marketeer, a tall, bubbly blonde with an exuberant laugh. Trying to be friendly, she once asked him the name of Hinduism's founder and the age of the Hindu Bible. Her clothes appear two sizes too small and she seems to enjoy her idle banter with all sorts of men who stop by her desk. Ved mostly avoids her.

One of Ved's neighbours is a soft-spoken older man in business development. He is very fond of saying 'partner or perish.' Among the books on his shelf are *The Tao of Business*, *Ten Laws of Leadership*, *Spiritual America* (on Native American shamans), and one that he insisted Ved must read: *The Monk Who Sold His Ferrari*. Ved began reading it but thought it was painfully misguided. His troubles began with the title itself. Why did the monk have a Ferrari at all? What exactly is so great about selling a Ferrari? Anyone can *sell* his Ferrari. Why didn't the monk just give it away? The rest of the book went steeply downhill from there.

Ved works in Omnicon's Business Security Division (or BS Division). His product line protects networked computers from viruses and worms, and he participates in dense debates on its evolution. His colleagues exhibit an entire gamut of instincts. From conservative advocates of incremental change to radicals inclined to ruffle things up. He can spot the ones addicted to the thrill of change and disruption as an end in itself—from smooth-talking executives to longhaired technocratic hipsters who sound deep, dream of changing the world through hi-tech, and love sci-fi flicks in which the hero, usually a white American man, saves the day for planet earth. Most of them see the world through the fog of trendy ideas and management theories *du jour*, attend workshops on leadership skills, build political factions and pour massive energy into life at work.

Ved is no fan of those who act irresponsibly or shirk commitments, but he has mixed feelings about such folks who take their jobs too seriously. On the one hand, he relies on their diligence and sincerity, and for this, he is grateful, but whenever he tries to enter their minds to see the world from within, he is invariably disenchanted. They may be the most analytical, ambitious, results-oriented people wrought by the churn of the corporate ocean, but they seem so naively optimistic about history and society, and they see technology as an uncomplicated force for good. Consumed by their daily exercises of petty egos and ambitions, do they ever wonder how ephemeral their lives are, how marginal to the blind will of the cosmos? Some surely must, but they hide themselves from him well enough.

They love to carry on about changing the world. But what sort of change? Indeed, what do they even know about the world that they want to change? Nothing Ved has learned about his colleagues gives him much confidence. So many live in a bubble, complacent in the belief that their way of life will be the one to prevail in the world.

One thing Ved likes about the system he is part of is that it creates new vocations, conveniences, and leisure through advances in technology, a quest as old as humankind. Yes, on a macro level, Silicon Valley is indeed advancing technology, even though it's organized to do so mainly for its own sake—by chasing money-making opportunities wherever they lead, rather than trying to solve the pressing problems of humanity. Yet, even when, despite itself, Silicon Valley helps solve the pressing problems of humanity, at a micro level Ved sees it brimming with un-heroic, pompous and self-centred gold-diggers. They are all around him, and they come from all over the world. Even the most articulate industry leaders, he finds, have remarkably naive views of the human material, laced with a self-serving techno-utopian optimism. That social good can result from their collective exertions is indeed a paradox of sorts.

And doesn't Silicon Valley amplify social inequalities? Doesn't it run on a libertarian ethos that justifies the rich getting richer, based on abstract technical skills like his own, which didn't even exist two decades ago? Nowhere else are there so many brattish billionaires. Through Omnicon, is he not helping a small class of techno-elites expand its power to shape the rest of humanity—how they socialize, learn and amuse themselves? What behaviours and values are their seductive innovations silently advancing? Haven't they made the pace of social change and dislocation faster than ever before? God knows what these gizmos and games are doing to our psyches. What ideas of 'us' and 'them', self and other, and habits of mind will they fortify? Is there anything more than a tenuous relationship between material and moral progress? Such thoughts come to him often and unbidden.

§

He walks to the kitchen for his afternoon cup of tea. He passes 'the accounting babe,' as Ravi calls her. A first-generation migrant from the Philippines, she is, according to Ravi, dating the recently divorced Director of Alliances. Further down, Ved pauses to make small talk with Scott, an engineer passionate about high-altitude camping. Last summer he had a close encounter with a grizzly bear in the Rockies, a story that practically everyone on their floor has heard.

Ved passes Ahmed, the only Arab-American on his floor. A while ago, a post-9/11 counter-terrorism drive in California required all Middle-Eastern Muslims to register and get fingerprinted. To his horror, Ahmed was among those detained for hours and questioned like a suspected terrorist. Hundreds were detained for minor visa violations. Some were forced to stand all night for lack of room, many were shackled and verbally abused, a few were even consigned to cold cells. Ahmed felt so humiliated by that experience that ever since then, it seems to Ved, he has had the besieged look of a hunted animal.

In the kitchen he runs into Elysia, a project manager. Earlier in the day, she had led a rather contentious End of Life meeting for a product. 'I thought your plan was perfect,' Ved says.

She blushes, 'Thanks, I did the best I could. Building consensus in that group is so hard.' He likes her soft, breathy voice and her Mediterranean looks. As she reaches above for a new box of sugar, he steals a glance at her breasts swaddled in a lacy bra under a semi-translucent blouse. Is she aware of his eyes on her, he wonders, as women are said to be?

'Did you hear our earnings announcement?' she asks.

'No, but let me guess, we missed our numbers again.'

'Yes, by a wide margin. The stock will tank on Monday.'

'Wasn't Greg able to spin it this time?' Ved chuckles.

'He tried. He was surprisingly upbeat. He talked about low channel inventories, healthy backlogs, and a robust pipeline. But the analysts on the earnings call seemed skeptical.'

A few months ago, Ved got into an argument with Elysia over a world map outside her cube, which showed America in the center and Asia split into two halves across the left and right edges. When he, in a good-humoured tone, offered to replace it with a 'proper map', she was genuinely puzzled. 'What's wrong with this one?'

'World maps are different outside the US,' he explained, 'more in line with historical developments in cartography—Europe in the middle, America on the left, and Asia on the right—depicting East and West visually.'

She got defensive and failed to see his point about how this was America indulging in its own glorification. 'I'm so used to this projection. Most Americans use it in school—it's just another map!' Ved had to drop the matter to avoid further aggravation.

Compared to these philistines and frogs in the well at Omnicon, Ved thinks, Liz is so refreshingly different. He is already looking forward to his second date with her tomorrow and a whole new experience for him—a ballet at the War Memorial Opera House.

Five

THEY STROLL THROUGH THE WAITING hall and basement café at the Opera House. Everyone seems dressed for the occasion. Liz too is wearing a stylish black dress and a colourful silk scarf. Ved is glad he threw on a coat at the last minute, else he would have stood out for sure.

Lights dim, the orchestra begins. Spry young people in lavish green costumes appear on stage. His eyes follow the lead dancer, his body language, expressions and acrobatics, as their dance turns into an energetic blur. So demanding yet so silly, he thinks, this vain preoccupation with body and youth. The costumes change across the opera's three divertissements, from green to red to sparkling white. He enjoys the music but dislikes all the pomp, the infantile glitter, the synchronized choreography. While he finds great beauty and delight in watching birds and fishes move in mesmerizing concert and formations, he finds it tedious when humans attempt the same, aiming for an obsessive perfection as an end in itself. It vaguely reminds him of military marches—a prejudice, he concedes, but one that he cannot easily shake off.

He finds his gaze slithering down all too often to the bony crotches of the ballerinas. He is amused by the thought that under the dignified rubric of art and culture, so many middle-aged men in the audience too are savouring their ethereal, prepubescent-looking bodies, maintained unnaturally at who knows what cost. He finds the spectacle both sad and comical—years of hard training for such little gain. Sort of like the masters of Hindustani classical vocals, with their absurd voice control and verbal calisthenics, fawning apprentices, and well-heeled socialites soaking in music and 'high culture'. But why single them out, he concedes, when obsessive, self-regarding toil is so common, from ancient Egyptians down to the employees of Omnicon?

'Wow, that was amazing,' Liz declares as they walk to his car. 'What did you think?'

'Quite a spectacle! More for the senses, though. Not much for the mind to latch on to.'

'I have this suspicion that you prefer intellectual delights to sensual ones.'

'Not always,' he smiles, 'I am all for sensual delights.'

She laughs, 'You know what I mean, that you tend to prefer analysis to feeling.'

'I think analysis is good. It enriches feeling, increases pleasure.'

'So your instinct is to analyze everything first?'

'Often, I suppose...I think I let analysis and feelings coexist, and inform each other.'

'How about no analysis, only feelings? Getting swayed by the mood, losing yourself?'

'Oh, I do that too sometimes, but I also tend to be sceptical of the senses.'

'Like today?'

'Yes, maybe so. Perhaps more so because I didn't

grow up watching ballets. So I instinctively turn up my analysis. You might do the same with Chinese opera, or some forms of Indian theatre.'

'Fair enough,' she concedes.

'I think of it this way—recently I came across this wonderful metaphor for the human psyche. Imagine a zoo with a zookeeper and lots of animals, wild and domestic, ferocious and meek, whose well-being depends on the zookeeper's knowledge of their unique characteristics. If he slouches off, the animals might suffer, or might turn on each other, and the overall health of the zoo suffers.' He looks at her and she nods.

'The animals represent the subterranean forces within us—the source of our feelings, passions, imagination. The zookeeper represents the rational faculty, drawn to analysis, order, classification. Both are part of who we are. Together they make up our psyche, or soul if you prefer. The zookeeper may study or regulate the animals, but may not tamper with their natures to avoid unpleasant side-effects. Part of his job is to also give meat to the leopards, feed bananas to the monkeys, and make many other arrangements—all for the health of the zoo. You can extend the metaphor further; for example, the animals inhabit constrained spaces, much like the effect our social conditioning has on our psyche.

'So that's what I mean when I say analysis and feelings coexist. I want to be led by an analytical faculty that worries about its own limits, knows when to humbly step aside and let feelings do their work, and inform the analysis. The health of my inner zoo depends on their fruitful coexistence and collaboration.'

'Hmm, fascinating,' Liz says softly. 'Sounds like you have it pretty well mapped out.'

'Does it?' he chuckles. 'But how it all works in practice is always more mysterious.'

He opens the passenger side door first. They're going to China Town for dinner.

§

They drive through an area with red curtained massage parlours and hookers pacing the streets. They stop at a red light behind a BMW. A hooker approaches its curbside window, talks to the driver, and hops in. Ved notices Liz shaking her head in what appears to be disapproval.

'Consenting adults,' he reminds her.

'You don't need to tell me that,' she says sharply.

'Why the disapproval then?'

'Because it's so sad, I just wish these women had other options.'

'Maybe they do. Are they doing this against their will here in San Francisco?'

'Just because they do this, quote-unquote, voluntarily, doesn't mean they do it because they are happy to. It's because they don't recognize, or lack, other options. Or they are addicted to abuse, or full of self-loathing and given to self-destruction.' Her voice bristles as she continues, 'It doesn't mean they like it, or choose it with a healthy frame of mind.'

'But if they do it voluntarily—so let's exclude the drug addicts—can we say we know better? Who should be allowed to save people from themselves? So many others don't like their jobs either, or choose them with a healthy frame of mind. I have met…'

She sighs, 'I know that line of reasoning, but taking a job flipping burgers is not quite comparable to letting a horny customer finger your private parts.'

'But many still choose the latter. They may not want to be saved, or pitied as victims of exploitation.'

'Listen,' she raises her voice, 'I don't know what the solution is. I just wish things were different, okay? All I'm saying is that prostitution springs from socioeconomic disadvantage and serious emotional problems. It exploits all kinds of women weakened by their circumstances, not just the drug addicts.'

'I agree with that, but wouldn't prostitution be around whether or not we like it? All we can do is try to minimize the crime and abuse and diseases associated with it, and treat it like a regular services sector job, as they do in parts of Europe.'

'Yes, I also believe in legalization. I think it's better for the women.' She resumes after a pause, her voice charged with emotion, 'At the end of the day, I guess, for me, it really comes down to how each of us projects our sexual power in the world and the kind of world it creates. What bothers me most about prostitution, to put it bluntly, is the way men approach sex.'

She continues, 'I might as well tell you right now that this is my hot-button issue—a personal hang-up—that sex ought to be shared respectfully. I think these women must die a little bit every day. Do you know what it's like dealing with foul manipulation, degrading language, being reduced to a mere sex toy by strangers, and even by men one has known and trusted? Do you know what it feels like to be *used*? You don't, you can't, because you are a man.'

He wants to say: We all have different thresholds of desecration and violation; your own thresholds are not universal. Don't rashly conflate paid sex with disrespect. Even in conventional unions—of lovers and spouses—payment for sexual favours, negotiated a lot less openly, occurs in other unsavoury forms. At least this is more honest and clear-cut. But he remains silent. He cannot dispel the whiff of a loophole in his reasoning.

Without warning, she begins to sob. He is dismayed by this development. He wasn't expecting tears on their second date. Who knows what history provokes this? He extends his right arm and gently squeezes her shoulder.

'I'm sorry,' she pulls a napkin from her bag, wipes her eyes, and then blows her nose into it. 'With some men, even I have felt like I'm beheld by eyes that belong to another kind of creature, who cannot see me in here. They only see what they want to see, which is not nearly who I am. I am a means to their sexual ends. Women have sexual needs too, you know, why can't men control themselves like we do? Why do they have to be so cavalier, so...'

Unthinking, preying, sordid...he silently shuffles the words. So true, and how curious that we once placed ourselves a step below the angels. He recently dwelled on the fact that each day so many men rape women, that one in six American women have apparently been raped at least once. For the first time recently, he had tried to imagine himself inside the mind of a rapist, how it operated—creative empathy one might say, and it filled him with revulsion for his sex. Such cruelty lurking just beneath the skin of men.

He knows he has it in him to reduce women's bodies to objects of pleasure, to imagine them as little more than *three holes and two hands*. Yes, yes, he knows that gaze. It's rooted in a primeval predatory force in him that he cannot wish away, only try to tame. Our religions too have long served to repress this gaze, but today's culture of individualism and popular porn, the so-called gonzo porn, thrives on and even cultivates this gaze. So many women in the business of porn now derive their livelihood from ordinary men—fathers, husbands, brothers, sons, uncles, neighbours, coworkers—exercising that gaze. How different is he from these men?

'I don't know how to defend this rationally,' she says, 'but I would feel emotionally unsafe with a lover who has frequented prostitutes. In a very personal, visceral way, I would feel hurt by the knowledge, somehow, knowing full well that it had nothing to do with me.' When he glances at her she is quietly staring out the window.

'I'm glad you're not like that,' she adds.

Not like what? Like the man in the BMW? He does not ask.

§

'Eew!' Liz exclaims as they walk past two large aquariums with live prawns, crabs, lobsters, and other creatures. They find a Szechwan restaurant with a large vegetarian selection. The waiter lights an oil lamp on their table. They order a beer each, hot and sour soup, eggplant in garlic sauce, wok-fried string beans, and steamed rice.

A television screen on mute shows footage from the Iraq War, then switches to an interview with Dick Cheney.

'That man is gross!' she snorts and gets all worked up. Led by ultra-conservatives, she rails, America has made the world a dangerous place with its naïveté, selfishness, and arrogant unilateralism. This rabble-rousing talk of evil and terror is, in reality, meant to fund a new imperium, a new Anglo-American empire.

'And who can fail to see the benefits of nukes?' she fumes. 'If the US is now building battlefield nukes—bunker busters they call them—why wouldn't every other country want its own nukes, so they can stop the yahoos of the Pentagon from fooling with them? Bloody hypocrites! The US is the only country that has actually used nuclear weapons. The world is rapidly going to hell in a handbasket,' she says, 'and it's going to end in a giant ball of fire.'

Towards the end of the meal Liz says, 'I'm quite a pessimist you know.'

'Oh really? You hide it so well.'

She laughs, 'What about you?'

'Neither a pessimist nor an optimist. I watch, I examine, without any preconceived notion, without any prepared idealism, and I am in no hurry to reach a verdict.'

'Ooh-la-la, that's original.' She looks amused.

'Well, not quite. I stole that line from Herzen, the nineteenth-century Russian philosopher. He saw pessimists and optimists as brothers under the skin. Say, in being equally cavalier in their disregard for evidence that does not suit their purposes.'

He offers to pay for dinner again. She puts up a brief resistance, then jokes, 'I won't feel terrible because you work for them capitalist pigs. No seriously, thank you! I appreciate it.'

On the drive back to her car parked near the Opera House, she turns to him and says, 'I'm sorry I got carried away earlier today and cried. I rarely do that sort of thing.'

'No worries. We all have hot-button issues. It's better to talk about them.'

'I couldn't agree more. It's important to hit all the big issues up front, rather than letting them simmer and boil over later. I'm so glad you agree!' Seconds later, she points towards a nondescript building, 'That's where I took my yoga classes last year.'

'I have no experience with yoga,' he admits. 'My ex, Pooja, dragged me to her yoga studio a couple of times but I didn't care for it. I much prefer the gym.'

'Oh, well,' she gives him a look of pity. 'It's never too late to discover one's heritage. Meanwhile, I need to find a new yoga centre. I might try power yoga this time, to lose some weight.'

He imagines a floor full of women doing power yoga wrapped in form-fitting clothes that accentuate their buttocks and breasts. Here are twenty-first century Americans adapting yoga to their fast and furious world, armed with 'spiritual tonics' laced with ginseng and ginkgo biloba. Even as, seven seas away, Indians are welcoming the joys of conspicuous consumption into their own world.

'By the way,' she says, 'how about a hike in Muir Woods next Saturday?'

'I love Muir Woods, so yes! How about a Malabar curry later, at my place? With coconut milk, baby corns, mustard greens, bell peppers, and my patent-pending mix of Malabar spices.'

'Wow, that sounds super delicious. I guess we have a date!'

Before getting out at the curbside, she turns to him, leans over and plants a kiss on his right cheek adjacent to his lips, 'Goodnight.'

Not just a customary goodbye-kiss, he knows, feeling somewhat tingly. Where might this lead? Watching her cross the road, he feels both excited and amused.

§

Back home, he walks to the corner store for milk. He notices a poster in a storefront window: 'No More Blood for Oil!' Spanish words waft out of a produce store. He passes a young couple engaged in a heated argument.

He recognizes two of the many homeless people who frequent his neighbourhood. They lie on the pavement, swaddled in filthy blankets. 'Spare change, please.' A shame that there are so many beggars in this rich city of visionaries, innovators, and liberals. The tech gold rush and its libertarian lackeys in the city will only make things worse. He gives them two dollars each, led in part by his own guilt at having come out ahead in the lottery of birth, and partly because he thinks it furthers neighbourly goodwill.

Baldev, a buoyant, clean-shaven Sikh man owns the corner store and runs it with the help of two Mexicans. He came to the US as a political refugee, his passport being the torture marks on his back, inflicted, he claimed, by the Punjab police. This was long after the end of the Sikh separatist insurgency in India. The way he told his story made Ved suspect that he had lied to get asylum, but in such matters, it is hard to be sure.

Ved recalls the day, nearly four years ago, when Baldev had offered kaju barfis to all visitors to his store. He was celebrating his recent marriage in Punjab. That's when he had opened up to Ved about his personal history, showed him a few wedding pictures, and shared his refugee story. Within a year, he was distributing kaju barfis again, this time for the birth of his daughter. Clearly, thought Ved, the pair wasted no time during their honeymoon. His wife and daughter were then still in Punjab, awaiting the visas to come through.

Almost eighteen months later, Ved saw Baldev's wife, Rashmi, for the first time. She sat in a corner holding baby Anita. She had a plain but sweet face and fitted his stereotype of a small-town Punjabi girl. She is a housewife and hardly ever comes to the store.

Just weeks ago, Ved again ran into her and Anita, now three, on one of their rare visits to the store. Ved exchanged greetings with Rashmi, and affectionately ruffled the child's hair. He asked about her favourite candy and bought it for her. To his surprise, she threw it on the ground and went running down one of the aisles.

§

Back in his apartment, Ved calls his parents. 'Good news!' they say, 'our tourist visas have arrived.'

They'll be in San Francisco in less than three months. Otherwise, the call is like most other calls. His parents speak of the comings and goings of relatives who have become a little remote to him over the years. One by one, his cousins have married, begotten children, bought homes. He can barely keep straight the names in his ever-expanding family tree.

Since he has nothing tangible to show for straying from this path, except perhaps his career in a world-famous company in America, his parents live in a state of perennial chagrin. Frequently still, Mother pesters him about marriage. She calls it the last unfinished business of her life. He does his best to manage their hopes without dousing them. Today, Mother merely frets over his diet and health and exhorts him to exercise daily. Is he using that Ayurvedic hair oil she got him to stem his dreadfully rapid hair loss?

They're planning a pilgrimage to Vaishno Devi, another Hindu temple on a hill with a large simian presence. Hundreds of stone steps must be climbed barefoot to derive maximum spiritual gain. Even so, Ved considers their religiosity relatively liberal—they visit temples but accept that God is everywhere, has many forms, is not vindictive towards non-believers, and makes no exclusive claims for a people. He has seen them turn more devout in old age. Why disapprove, he reckons, if it helps ease their passage to the great oblivion? We all need such tricks, in our own separate ways.

Six

VED STARTS HIS WEEK AT work trapped in a workshop on process quality. Their instructor Jim is an animated man from Omnicon's Dallas office, with jiggling rolls of fat around his waist and a preachy tone laced with verbal tics: umm, so, all righty. Most of the dozen-odd attendees appear bored and, like Ved, seem to be attending only to satisfy management directives.

During lunch, Jim devours a quarter pound of roast beef while relating real-world process quality case studies in his Texan accent. Back in class after lunch, Ved asks him a question on one of the case studies. Jim nods, considers it for a few seconds, and then quite abruptly requests a member of the audience to step out of the room with him. This seems odd to Ved. He follows them a minute later to find Jim stretched out on a table in the hallway, panting, hands on chest, forehead slick with sweat, complaining of pain radiating out to his arms and shoulders.

The building security officer has already called the paramedics. Jim steadies his breath briefly and asks to speak to his wife on his phone. 'Honey, I have chest pains again, I might be going to the hospital. No, no, I'll be fine. I'll call you later.'

Ved removes Jim's shoes and helps to loosen his tie,

then rushes to get some water. Others have come out of the classroom, but no one seems to know what to do; they stand around looking alarmed.

The paramedics arrive within minutes, loosen his clothes, check his vital signs, ask him about his medications and administer oxygen from a tube. A heart attack, someone whispers. The diagnosis unsettles Ved. He tries to relate to Jim's struggle for life: the cold and the dread, the physical convulsions. Did his question trigger the attack? The paramedics rush him to the hospital. Ved is once again impressed by the efficiency and professionalism of emergency medical services in America. The workshop is adjourned.

Next morning an email from Jim's divisional VP announces that Jim, forty-nine, passed away in his sleep. The news jolts Ved. Jim's family took the last flight out of Dallas but arrived too late. He will be greatly missed, says the VP. Those affected by this tragic loss can opt for company-paid grief counselling, whether in-person or by calling toll-free and speaking with Grief Counsellors who are standing by 24/7, a perk for all Omnicon employees.

Ved comes home early and goes out for a walk in his neighbourhood. At a busy square, he sits on a stone bench and watches people scurrying about with their cares and worries. He recalls that the last normal thing Jim did was to ponder his question on quality, before succumbing to the quality defects in his own design. One moment so full of life, the next moment a fish out of water, fluttering for dear life on an office table. 'The greatest wonder of all,' said Yudhishthira, 'is that each day death strikes, and we live as though we were immortal.'

What would he prefer more, Ved wonders: to face death in full awareness down to the last breath, or dying unexpectedly in sleep some night? He imagines himself dead yet watching the world. He imagines his own funeral, his body upon a pyre, flesh and bone crackling in a fire fuelled by ghee. From earth to earth, ashes to ashes, dust to dust. All at once, he feels unmoored, cast adrift upon the blind, mystifying will of nature.

§

Next morning, Ved gets an email from Ravi. Things have apparently moved faster than Ravi expected. He is going to India in a week to meet potential brides—his parents' shortlist has at least three promising candidates. With some luck, he will return with one. The same day, they go out to a Thai restaurant for lunch. Ved mentions Jim's death.

'Life is like software man,' Ravi turns philosophical, 'an endless fucking upgrade cycle, with a fatal system crash in the end. Sometimes I wish I had the guts to quit this madhouse we work in, and retreat to an ashram in the Himalayas.'

'Think again. No booze or babes in those ashrams. And when your balls freeze in the cold, you'll only find hairy babas to massage them.' They both laugh.

Ravi then rails about a colleague in advertising, 'You won't believe the tagline she chose for my product: "For Zen Like Calm". Bloody airhead! The ad shows an engineer in a meditative trance next to our ugly hardware. All she creates is noise and corny messages.'

'Relax man, the world is full of people for whom

corny messages actually work,' Ved chuckles. 'In your job, this attitude won't take you far. Here is some unsolicited advice: pick your battles carefully. These resentments accumulate.' Ravi calms down a bit.

It is the season of performance reviews at Omnicon, and Ravi has just finished his. Ved's own is due in a week. Ravi not only confirms that there will be no raises or promotions this year, but he also suspects major changes in the weeks ahead: perhaps a 'reorganization'—euphemism for layoffs—in light of Omnicon's revenue shortfall for two consecutive quarters.

'Did your manager offer any clues?' asks Ved.

'No. I don't think he knows much either. He just echoed what his manager told him: tighten your seatbelt. Personally, I think your product line is not as vulnerable as mine.'

'Depends on whom you ask. We are falling behind in features and losing market share. A virus duped our antivirus software last month and infected five big customer networks, including Goldman Sachs. We got terrible press for that.' They eat in silence for a while.

'You know,' says Ravi, 'I've been thinking about this lately, that in some huge ways, this whole country revolves around selling—a nation of fuckin' salespeople! Selling gizmos, fashion, democracy, weapons, sex, management theories, you name it! The sales mentality is so fuckin' pervasive, don't you think?'

'Yeah, I agree with you. Napoleon had similar words for the British of his day, "a nation of shopkeepers". In America, I think the obsession with winning and getting ahead, sometimes at steep personal and social costs, has become deeply ingrained in too many people.'

Ravi mulls this over, then declares, 'I don't feel like going back. My afternoon is packed with meetings on branding and messaging. All the usual honchos into power trips will be there, all hell-bent on protecting their fiefdoms—doing the right thing has become an afterthought. Pisses me off big time.'

'Ah, yes, power trips, but the only way to entirely avoid power trips is to retreat in solitude to the Himalayas. Even with one other person involved, there is a power trip.'

'I'm telling you man, all roads lead to the Himalayas,' Ravi laughs. 'But tell me how you put up with all this shit, man? I get flustered and get into these irritating arguments that go nowhere. They turn into battles of will. I hardly ever see you flustered.'

'I suspect you take things too seriously. Let go a bit. Focus on the important stuff. Don't make it personal. Check your ego outside the meeting room.'

He must sound like those vapid management gurus, Ved realizes, but keeps going. 'I often see each power trip as a theatrical act, and I watch it unfold through a person's rank, tone of voice, eyes, body language. It is fun to watch people with a bit of detachment, to see them as specimens of humanity. We all do this to some extent but do it more consciously next time.'

'How will that help me get what I want?' Ravi sounds impatient.

'Insight into others is a form of knowledge, a source of power. If you understand what others fear and admire, what stokes their egos, and what motivates them, you can then use this knowledge to your advantage.'

'How? Give me an example,' Ravi persists.

'Imagine a colleague. Ask him about something that's important to him: health, family, vacation, sports, or something at work. Try to win his trust, show that you take him seriously and give his point of view some thought. Address his or her concerns, rather than using emotion or logic to only push for what you want. Lo and behold, you'll find doors opening for you, people yielding to your point of view, or willing to make compromises—Salesmanship 101, essential for climbing all ladders. Of course, some do this better than others. I am not good at it myself.'

Ved cannot tell whether Ravi is bored or lost in thought. 'Tell me about your India trip.'

'My parents have lined up some interesting babes, man,' Ravi says. 'Fingers crossed.'

'Sounds like reverse swayamvara,' Ved teases. Ravi is not entirely at ease with arranged marriage but has sufficiently rationalized it in his mind. He even echoes a few homilies: as many arranged marriages turn out happy as love marriages; convenience is as good a reason to marry as love; convenience can lead to love just as often as love can sour into inconvenience.

However, a little problem remains: no one in Ravi's group knows about his marriage plan. He doesn't know how to break it to them. Most Americans won't understand it, nor will they respect him for it. They will ask awkward questions or avoid the topic entirely. But he doesn't need to deal with it until after his return. Besides, there is always a chance that nothing will work out and he will return empty-handed.

'Go strike 'em dead, champ,' Ved says in the parking lot at Omnicon.

'Thanks, man. May the force be with me,' he grins. 'See you in three weeks.'

§

News arrives that Technocon, their main rival, has acquired a startup and entered the hot new space of web traffic monitoring. Folks in Ved's BS Division are alarmed. Omnicon has a similar product and this alters the playing field. Their salespeople are jittery and need urgent guidance. His VP convenes an emergency staff meeting to discuss the event and prepare an official response.

Hours later, a communiqué to the employees of his division calls the news a decisive validation of Omnicon's strategy. Technocon's move will serve to educate the marketplace, thereby benefiting Omnicon in the long run—the market will simply choose the better product, namely Omnicon's. It exaggerates both its own strengths and Technocon's weaknesses. Ved has seen this before and watches all the hoopla, denial, and spin with familiar tedium.

At times, he likens his workplace to a medieval monastery, with its own formal language, etiquette, dense disputations, half-truths and plain lies. It has a hierarchy and basis of ascension, secret intrigues and politics—stomping grounds for the irrepressible human ego. But at least he understands this world, and the disputations are mostly collegial and decorous, especially at his level, where the stakes are not too high. Despite its many discontents, there is still an idea of order, a common sense of purpose. Despite himself, he derives a numbing comfort from it.

§

Liz calls him at home in the evening. She has dramatic news: a major exodus has happened at her non-profit group. Many of her colleagues have quit to set up a brand new, for-profit company that will rate consumer products across additional environmental metrics. 'It'll make their services more attractive to corporate customers. They are trying to recruit me too.'

'What additional metrics?' Ved asks.

'Take an article of clothing. Besides the fabric and materials used—natural, recycled, synthetic—they might also rate the longevity of the garment, its strength, drying time, the labour employed, or any problems arising in its disposal due to the type of dye used.'

'Are you going to join them?'

'It's tempting, you know. I'll get a raise and stock options; I'll finally be able to pay off my student loans. But I also believe they won't be able to stay unbiased. They'll be led by profit and shareholder returns, and to justify their subscription fees, they'll feel pressured to make their large clients look good. I don't want to be a part of that.'

'Oh, that's so familiar to me. When we want a case study, we hire an "objective and independent" firm to produce what we want to hear about our product—we don't go for total lies, but we want partial, selective truth. Or else, the agency doesn't get repeat business and we don't publish their findings.' While talking to her, he pours himself a cup of sake.

Liz prides herself for having avoided corporate America in her sixteen years of work. She has remained true to her ideals, she says. She must not cave in now and begin her descent into that abyss of narrow self-interest. Corporations, like wild beasts, are led by blind appetites—for profit in their case—and nothing beyond. This may make them efficient, but it also makes them inhumane. Even politicians are now in cahoots with them, rather than checking their toxic impact on society. Checks and balances are eroding fast...the whole edifice is rotten...

Ved listens as she reiterates her views on the ethics of corporations and the mercenary mindset of those who work there. She pauses to note that there are exceptions, of course, Ved being one. This corporate capitalism creates its own impetus for war, she says. The economic elites—corporate shareholders all—only care about the interests of their own class. No wonder two-thirds of global arms exports come from American corporations.

Ved regrets his part in getting her started on this topic again. Not that he disagrees, but he struggles with the relentless griping and pessimism in her rants.

Several minutes later, she asks, 'Hey, would you like to join me and a friend on Friday for dinner in the city, followed by an evening at a Latin dance club? It'll be great fun!'

Does she want to get her friend's opinion on him, to spot any glaring problems that she herself doesn't see? 'Thanks, but I'm meeting my college buddies that evening. Also, just so you know this about me, I prefer to dance in private. I'm not into dance floors full of sweaty bodies gyrating to deafening noises. And what's up with all those silly strobe lights?'

'Ah-ha, we'll have to work on reforming that pompous attitude.' They laugh together. Before saying goodbye, they confirm their hike and dinner plan for Saturday.

He lights a candle, dims all other lights, and plays an album of West African acoustic music that he recently acquired. He likes its refreshing earthiness, the simple, lilting beats, the weathered baritone. Two more drinks later, light-headed, he rises to dance in his pajamas: undulating hips and shoulders, slow and fluid, shadow limbs casting patterns on the wall.

§

On Thursday morning he flies to Los Angeles to present at Omnicon's Annual West Coast Seminar. His job is to introduce both new and upcoming features of his product. With luck, a few would sign up for evaluations, followed by a purchase.

He has done dog-and-pony shows throughout his career. He knows his material well. His audience is staid middle managers from corporate America. All at once, he feels detached, cold. Who are these people? He could not care less for them, or for his product. His audience might as well be chimps and he an orangutan, set to perform for each other. Try hard as he might, he cannot swing back into the act. Images of chimps and orangutans keep flashing in his mind.

A part of him is distraught. He has been slumping

into this state of uncaring all too often lately—an all-pervading desire to be elsewhere, like a caged bird longing for the sky.

Predictably, he doesn't make a good impression. His opening joke falters. He runs through his material mechanically; his lack of enthusiasm shows. The audience reviews at the end are bad. He scores either at par or below other speakers. Some have even scribbled critical remarks: humdrum presentation; speaker lacked passion for his product; more pizzazz needed. Take the cue, he tells himself, quit this line of work before it turns you into a total zombie.

Flying home with him is Steve, a product manager from his division. Before the flight, Steve drags him to an airport bar where he orders a double martini and a huge platter of grilled tiger prawns. Steve's successful battle with stage three colon cancer, now in remission, inspired him to return to his job—not for money, but for the love of building new things, and for the 'awesome pace and excitement' of the hi-tech industry.

Steve takes his work seriously, studies its laws, protocols, and secret handshakes. His conspiratorial mind revels in doomsday scenarios for data security: hackers, criminals and cyberpunks are becoming smarter; many are aligning with terror networks; major disruption and chaos in America are closer than we think. This message of course works well to sell Omnicon's security products—perhaps why most colleagues, who dislike him otherwise, tolerate him. He rarely takes vacations and sends work emails at odd hours of the night. Fortunately for Ved, a baseball game on TV distracts Steve, curtailing conversation.

Ved drifts into his own reverie: what would he do if he had colon cancer and was given, say, a year to live? He would quit his job immediately. Visit the people and places of his past, especially in India. Live more lyrically and consciously. Arrange to donate all of his possessions. Above all, try to live without fear—but why isn't he doing this already? So full of fear is he, fear that he has even learned to rationalize—fear of committing to larger causes, of getting too close to people, of the unknown. 'Fear is not a disease of the body,' wrote Gandhi, 'fear kills the soul.' What is fear doing to his soul?

Across the aisle, he notices a skinny girl, barely fifteen. Based on her dress sense, she must surely be in thrall to a sexy pop diva. What a shame, Ved thinks, for girls to be sexualized this early in life. He steals a glance at her lacy panties exposed above her skimpy shorts. While averting his gaze, his eyes meet those of a man beside her, no doubt her father. Ved regrets it immediately. In merely an instant, a world of knowledge and emotions pass between them.

Seven

'YOU SHOULD LEARN FROM YOUR college friends,' his mother often says. 'Settled, all settled. What is so hard, why can't you be settled? Not one of them that has not given their parents grandchildren. But my son, no, my son is the one left with no family.'

'I'm busy,' Ved would mutter. 'I'm not ready for family-shamily yet.'

'See how he talks! Who isn't busy? Are your friends sitting at home doing nothing?'

On Friday, Ved meets these friends from his college years back in India: Balaji, Vikram and Sunil, who, if you asked his mother, had it all: the job; the house; the wife and children. Ved hasn't seen them in weeks. Balaji's wife and children are visiting India, so he offered to host this men-only evening. Booze and Indian snacks kick off the evening.

Conversation ranges across stocks, gadgets, restaurants, cricket, sundry batch-mates and industry news. Guy talk, he imagines Liz saying dismissively. When together, they all have a jolly good time with their college lingo, with its profanities, risqué humor, and the bawdy nicknames they had acquired. At the same time, Ved marvels at their much stronger nostalgia and appetites for jokes and anecdotes that hark back to their teenage years. It's as if a part of them refuses to grow up.

'You look depressed, man,' Balaji says, trying to rouse Ved. 'Drink up! The first one should go down fast.' Balaji is VP of Marketing in a 900-person software company. Of the four of them, he has risen the highest on the corporate ladder. Even in college, he was the confident and dynamic kind, more ambitious than the rest. Then, too, his dream was to be a captain of the industry. He even reviewed business books for a campus magazine; now he blogs about business books, industry news, technology trends, movies and cricket.

'This bugger has changed so much, hasn't he?' says Vikram, referring to Ved. Vikram is the lead product architect at a computer networking startup and an authority on technical matters that few in the world could comprehend. Last year, his company filed multiple patents for his routing algorithms. Alas, the IPO market has cooled off and, to his chagrin, he must wait for his big bucks. Then, like Balaji, he too will retreat to the hills, to gorgeous views of the bay, the best school district and the envy of fellow Indians. What a journey for a shy young man from Varanasi who, as a college freshman, was guilt-ridden and paranoid about damaging his health from excessive masturbation. What worried him then was his belief that forty drops of blood went into making a drop of semen, which meant that soon he would have little blood left.

'I know what he is thinking. He is plotting another escape into virtual reality,' Sunil teases, referring to Ved's penchant for 'third world' travel. Sunil seems to have made peace with a tech-support job and life in a leafy middle-class suburb. He came to the US only six years ago and fits the desi geek stereotype: an earnest, diffident, god-fearing man who keeps the gears of US technology turning. In college, his nickname was Pujari, because in their freshman year he had hung images of buxom goddesses in his room—and prayed to them. The calendars came down after the brutal teasing he got but the name stayed. Of the three, he is the most laidback, with a dreamy detachment from his life and times, disinclined to venture his opinion on the issues of the day.

'Dudes, I'm listening!' Ved forces a laugh at their nodding, shaking heads. 'That, too, is part of a conversation.' He's glad that they don't launch into one of their favourite ways of pulling his leg by making fun of his vain obsession with his hairstyle and clothes in college. The softly playing songs of Kishore Kumar suddenly fill Ved with a nameless longing for India.

Balaji mentions a former colleague, a white man around their age, who has just retired to pursue music, having struck gold a couple of years ago in his company's IPO. Balaji and Vikram debate how much money one needs for early retirement in the US. Their estimates are five times higher than Ved's. The topic shifts to the booming call-centre market in India. 'Multinationals are stampeding to get there,' Balaji bristles with pride. 'What poetic justice! Our English language skill, a legacy of British rule, is now stealing jobs away from Britain.'

Vikram and Sunil chime in, the mood is upbeat. First-world lifestyles have come to India. Indians have acquired a whole new sense of pride and self-confidence.

Out with the depressing Western obsession with ash-smeared fakirs, poverty, filth, disease, caste, bride burning and communal violence. In with the nukes, IT, high GDP growth, global goods and services, award-winning novelists and beauty queens. They have bought into the Bharatiya Janata Party's 'India Shining' slogan. 'The sleeping tiger,' proclaims Vikram, 'has awakened at last!'

So much has changed since they went their own ways after college. What they have most in common—memories from a formative past—keeps fading into irrelevance. But their bonds were forged in the trenches, so to speak, where they saw each other's deepest vulnerabilities—bonds still visible in the ease of their interactions. Among them, despite their divergent views and priorities in life, Ved still finds a measure of camaraderie and comfort in their familiar faces. He can talk about some things only among them or make the goofiest of jokes. They are among those one considers lifelong friends. He can call for their help and respond to their call without hesitation. Tracking their paths also helps him calibrate his own journey in life.

Their college was one of the best in India. Many of his classmates, including him, won financial aid from graduate schools in the US. It was all anticipation back then; a world of novel experiences and untold pleasures of the flesh awaited them in America. Looking back, it's clear to Ved that this was based on little more than India's own stereotypes of America, fuelled by pop culture and the imaginings of porn.

They had arrived in Silicon Valley after stints of various lengths in other parts of the US. As far as he knows, none of these three has ever 'fucked a white chick', something which they'd all fantasized about back then. Each had gone back home for an arranged marriage in his own caste community, ending the torment of loneliness and unrequited desires.

Ved thinks they secretly envy his single life and travels, and the sexual adventures they suspect he often has with exotic women from around the world. That might explain why, other than an occasional query, they don't probe this part of his life. He does nothing to combat their suspicion—in their minds, it likely takes the shine off their more conventional successes.

When they regrouped in Silicon Valley more than a decade after graduation, Ved noticed how much they had slipped into a tedious domesticity. Together with their wives—women cute, clever and talented enough to land husbands in America—they now indulge their middle-class yearning for prestige and status through cars, furniture, luxury cruises, home theatres, and decorative kitsch like Irish crystal, silk carpets and replicas of famous art. Ved has had to endure their long and nuanced conversations about this stuff.

Both husbands and wives now variously relate their fears of visiting India—what if their kids pick up some god-awful disease? They see deadly infections lurking everywhere. They fall for exaggerated urban legends about food adulteration rackets. Heaven forbid that they should rely on India's medical system. On their last visit, Vikram and his wife played it safe by hauling a suitcase full of packaged food, including even cartons of powdered milk. On their visits home, they now float above India's grime like brown sahibs: insulated by luxury, marvelling at its exotica, isolated by their class and deeply ingrained sense of social hierarchy.

Ved's own relationship with India has changed too but in different ways. He now sees its massive human diversity, identities, and contradictions, its layered and contested history, its complex struggles with modernity and markets, and even its cruelties and saving graces. Far from pride or chauvinism, he sees in India an amazing window into the human material, existing as if in multiple centuries at once. Every time he leaves the bubble of Silicon Valley and visits India, he feels alive in new ways. Ved has often thought of moving to India for an extended period and reconnecting with it at its own pace. But various fears, including the fear of uncertainty, keep him from doing so. Yet, more and more, he feels that by putting it off he is selling out, stagnating by choosing the safe and the bland, wasting the best years of his life doing someone else's bidding.

At the same time, Ved sees his friends and their wives turning into anxious immigrants and helicopter parents. Their next decade will go into chasing kids around a regimen of soccer, piano, chess, computers, Bharatnatyam, science fairs, math Olympiads, and trips to Orlando and grandparents in India. Add to this the hormone-fuelled battles with their teens across big cultural gulfs. They'll not only push their kids into STEM disciplines, they'll also push on them their social conservatism and disdain for the arts and the humanities. Coddled and overprotected, they may well become professional high-achievers and big earners, but would they ever undo the psychic damage from such controlling parenting? Ved's heart goes out to the kids. Good parenting is hard, he now realizes, and suspects that he too would've failed in his own ways. Watching their family dynamics, he often quietly celebrates steering clear of fatherhood.

Balaji and Vikram are even hardening into middling men of the Indian Right. While Balaji is more cerebral about his politics—he can hold forth on both Savarkar and Hayek, for instance—Vikram is cruder. Both oppose caste-based reservations and favour the 'merit' of test scores in jobs and education. Both support wholesale privatization of the Indian economy and the Hindu nationalist party with its macho stance on national defense and terrorism. Vikram likes the BJP for stopping 'our pandering to the Muslims. It's simple, yaar, if the Muslims don't like it in India, they can go to Pakistan, breed all they want, and freely cheer for their cricket team too.' More recently, he spoke about the Shock and Awe attack on Baghdad with a mix of envy and admiration.

Ved cannot recall any early signs of such attitudes from their college days. Balaji and Vikram now hold that the ancient Aryan migration into India is a myth cooked up by prejudiced colonial historians, whose work is now carried forward by their brainwashed Indian acolytes, the so-called sepoys, in the left-liberal academy. The Harappans, they believe, spoke a precursor language to Sanskrit, the oldest, most perfect language in the world—naturally, their Hindu ancestors' gift to humanity.

What experiences, wonders Ved, led them down this track of cultural insecurity and chauvinism? Clearly, new forces of self and identity now coursed through them. In the last couple of years, they've acrimoniously debated these topics. Unlike in college, when the bitter aftertaste of their debates was short-lived, the bitterness now lingers and colours their friendship. Who was that famous author who saw in every friendship an inconspicuous drama, a series of subtle wounds? Ved once felt so much closer to them and shared so many common joys, fears and concerns. Now he relates less and less to their values and aspirations in life—a loss that he tries to be stoic about in his lucid moments.

Some months ago, Vikram casually lamented that Ved had become 'too American', which Ved takes as code perhaps for too individualistic, too much of a California liberal, with too many un-Indian tastes and manners. Balaji and Sunil agreed, without saying why. Even their wives regard him with some frostiness, not the least because of his breakup with Pooja. He can imagine them saying behind his back, 'Ooh baba, how can he be so cold towards his own biological child?'

His interactions with the wives now rarely go beyond polite banter or mundane topics. When he thinks of them and their kids-centric domesticity, he drolly thinks of having 'dodged that bullet'—all reasons why the time spent with his friends has organically reduced.

§

Balaji has cooked palak paneer and a spicy dum aloo with tortillas and rice. The food tastes even better in their drunken state. After dinner, Ved pulls out a marijuana joint that Sasha had left him weeks ago. Sunil cheers but Vikram and Balaji resist and have to be cajoled into joining. They spread out sleeping bags on the carpet, dim the lights, smoke and reminisce nostalgically over coconut and cashew barfis. They recall the night when they got stoned and jumped the walls of their college pool for a swim, only to be caught pants-down by the watchman; and the night when their uptight hostel warden busted their blue film screening. Sunil breaks into a pot-induced giggle and is soon joined by others. It is well after midnight when they call it a night. Ved slips into a sleeping bag and quickly falls asleep into a dream.

He arrives at work to find a yellow note stuck on his computer screen. It is from his divisional VP, 'Please see me at once'. He rushes across a bustling street thronging with people, cycle-rickshaws, hawkers, stray dogs, garishly painted auto-rickshaws, and climbs three flights of stairs to reach the VP's office. It overlooks the lush green lawns of a British era bungalow. Peacocks caw now and again. The VP's sexpot secretary receives him with a smile, 'There you are, Vade! We've been waiting for you.'

'Hell-low Ved!' the VP greets him, 'Come in, come in. Take a seat!'

Ved is taken aback by his enthusiasm. From behind his desk in the middle of the room, the VP points to the only chair across him. Above the desk hangs a bulb with a conical lampshade. There are no other lights. But this is not a private meeting. Many of Ved's colleagues are seated in the low light along three walls. They look at him intently as he scans the room. What occasion might warrant this assembly?

'I will get to the point right away,' the VP says in a

businesslike tone. 'We are all adults here, aren't we?' He leans forward, stares into Ved's eyes, and says, 'I know you're a terribly smart guy. Nobody here disagrees with that. But there is another fact nobody here disagrees with, that you don't care about this stuff at all, about what we do here at Omnicon, do you?'

Ved is taken aback. The VP continues, 'I've watched you for months, and listened to the feedback from your peers. I'm persuaded that you do this like an ordinary bloody job, don't you? It's as if you are biding your time. You would much rather be elsewhere, wouldn't you?'

Ved listens carefully to every word the VP speaks. He has long prepared for this moment but words elude him now. He mumbles defensively, 'Wait, that's not true, you know that's not true. I am responsible and trustworthy, more than most of your employees. I keep my promises. I care about my word to my colleagues. I...'

'Enough! I see it—it is evident on your face every day. Nothing at work motivates you. You seem to be in it only for the paycheck. You're totally burned out, not engaged enough, not ambitious enough.'

'But that's not true. In fact, you gave me a promotion and a raise last year.'

'That means nothing. You're smart enough to know that raises have become an entitlement around here. I tell you, this corporate socialism is killing us, destroying our competitiveness. But all along, I could see through your sham, your facade. No wonder you function far below your potential.'

'That's not true. I do what is expected of me. I pay attention...'

'Maybe you do, but you're not dedicated, like these men and women here. I need dedicated people.' With fingers taut, as if clutching an imaginary cricket ball, he slowly shakes his fist at him, 'You, in contrast, are without passion, without fire. That really is the bottomline.'

Ved looks around. His own manager, Roger, is curiously missing. Amid the stony faces are Steve and Elysia, and a smirking colleague whom he sparred with recently on Middle-Eastern politics. But deep down Ved knows the VP is correct. Ved's longstanding fear has come true—he has landed a VP who is totally committed to the corporate enterprise, who sees clearly, and who, like a mind reader, has now seen through him.

Ved tries to appear calm, 'Listen, I think there might be a bit of a...a perception gap...I don't promote myself well enough. I was never good at self-promotion. Give me time, I will work on filling this perception gap.' He hears low titters from the gallery.

'Ah-ha-hah, listen to that!' The VP casts a smile around the room. 'Our friend here says he will work on promoting himself, on filling "a perception gap". Pray tell me, why just the perception gap? Why not the enthusiasm gap, the dedication gap, the ambition gap?'

'At least the perception gap,' Ved mumbles. 'First perception, then the rest.' He immediately regrets saying that. He is digging a hole for himself. He resents the power he confers upon the VP with his weak, fudging ways. He is disgusted by his inability to fight like a man, to protest this public humiliation, to cast away his fear, boldly resign, and walk out with his head held high, donning the Buddha smile. Isn't that precisely what a self-respecting person should do? All his fond ideals and principles seem worthless in the light of this moment.

'Okay, out!' the VP gestures at the people along the walls. 'We are done. Now I need a private word with my friend here.' His tone is mocking, his smile sinister. Ved watches the room clear in seconds. Now it's only the two of them. Ved prepares for the hammer to fall.

Suddenly, Ved wakes up, sweating, breathing hard, with two snoring bodies next to him. He is still in his sleeping bag at Balaji's place. 'Phew,' he sighs with relief, falling back on the pillow. He rarely has anxiety dreams about his job. It stays with him the entire morning, as he drives home, bathes, and sets out to spend the day with Liz.

Eight

'My mom called yesterday. She wants me to go see her in Santa Cruz,' Liz reveals soon after they set out on a five-mile hiking trail amid old-growth redwood and sequoia trees.

'Great, next weekend hop in your car and go.' Ved takes in the soft, damp earth and the thick undergrowth that carpets the forest floor. Wildflowers and bright red berries abound. A mild breeze conveys the musky scent of the ocean.

'Well, this may come as a shock to you but I'm not too fond of my mother. She was horrible to me and my sister—absent, selfish, neurotic. She is the kind who shouldn't have kids. Now she's turned even more caustic and bitchy in old age. No wonder she has no friends. You know this is hard for me to say but if I were my father, I would've left her too.'

Liz sighs, 'But all said and done, I still love her. She is my mother and there is no one else to care for her. She is even starting to forget things—I feel sorry for her. My sister got off easy. She married a Canadian and escaped to Toronto years ago.' A look of annoyed resignation crosses her face. 'Now I'm stuck with my mother. And, tenacious as she is, she might live to a hundred.' She pauses, then adds, 'She doesn't even have a fortune to leave behind.'

Her father is much nicer, Liz says. Once an Adjunct Professor at a college in Santa Cruz, he now lives a retired life in southern California. But eight years ago, just before his retirement, he was disgraced in a plagiarism scandal and fired from the college. He never quite recovered from it, nor found another job. He moved south and now lives like a mole with his bickering bitch of a wife who doesn't like Liz. He drinks too much, and they barely make ends meet.

'Sorry to hear that,' he says, 'what a difficult situation.' A short silence ensues.

'You Indians are so lucky,' she says sombrely. 'Loving parents, focus on family and education, respect for tradition.' It strikes him that she has a rather sanitized view of Indian family life, probably owing to some sort of New Age sensibility that makes India seem nobler from afar.

She pauses to stare at a family of redwoods, 'Gosh, so tall, one can skydive from the top!' They spot a centipede and a scorpion scuttle across the path. She walks ahead of him on a narrow part of the trail. He watches her gait, rolling hips, the billowing black skirt, the chunky calves. He has never fondled a buttock that large.

The trail turns steeper. They climb in silence for a few minutes. She is adept at identifying trees. A tan oak here, and that's a madrone. Over there, by the big-leaf maple, is a Douglas fir. This scent is probably vanilla grass. He admits his ignorance of even the most common plants and trees.

'Did you know,' she asks, 'that Sequoia was a Cherokee chief who created the first Native American alphabet? That enabled the Cherokee people to read and write and soon led to a literacy rate higher than that of the surrounding white settlers.'

'Huh, I didn't know that.'

They stop and rest on a high ridge with a view of the Pacific Ocean. She pulls out oranges, granola bars, water and napkins from her daypack. They rest and eat.

'I love being out in nature,' she says. 'Lucky we still have this left. But at the rate we're going, can you imagine the earth in fifty years?' She shudders. 'If we could learn only one thing from the Native Americans, it'd have to be their view of nature's sacred balance, don't you think? They saw how everything is interconnected and lived in quiet harmony with nature. They didn't see it as a resource to be endlessly plundered for their own gain.'

'Nature's sacred balance? Can anything be sacred in the absence of God?'

'Not if one clings to a simple, anthropomorphic notion of God. But one can also understand God, as I do, to be more of a process, a design in which we participate. Eastern religions got it right: God pervades everything and is infinite. Sometimes I feel nature beckons me, as if...as if it were a divine oceanic womb. Have you ever felt that way?'

'Beckoned by a womb? Nope. Wombs strike me as clammy, uncomfortable places.'

'I should have guessed,' she laughs with him. 'There's not much hope for you. Have you no reverence for nature, for the life force that unites the world, makes it hum?'

'I have tremendous wonder for it, but not quite reverence. Nothing in nature cares about me, so why should I waste my reverence on it? Besides, why is there so much evil in nature? So much unfairness? So much suffering?'

'That's so Judeo-Christian, this talk of good and evil. Humans are parts of nature too; don't we care about each other? Aren't there other ways of understanding our existence? Life and nature are so much more mystical. We are still so clueless about the big questions: why is there something rather than nothing? Why do space, time and matter exist? Why did life and evolution come into being? Why is everything in nature so intricately connected? We know practically nothing, though we like to pretend otherwise.'

'Sure, we're clueless as you say, but being clueless need not lead to reverence. I'd rather figure out how to be less clueless, rather than retreat into reverence. How does that help?'

'It helps protect nature, no? Also keeps us humble and grounded.'

'Perhaps, but I prefer other, more rational and existential reasons for protecting nature, and for staying humble and grounded.'

A raven caws raucously. Leaves rustle in a gentle breeze. They drink water and watch the landscape in silence. An Indian couple appears on the trail. The man is wearing an ICC Cricket World Cup sweatshirt.

'Ah, cricket. Was there a cricket world cup recently?' she asks.

'Yeah. In South Africa.'

'My father loved cricket. He played it growing up in England. Aren't Indians quite good at it?'

'They are. That's about the only sport they are good at.'

'That's right,' she laughs, 'Indians are dreadful at sports. They hardly ever win anything at the Olympics. Why do you think that is?'

'Partly because India hasn't prioritized spending money on modern, high-tech training.'

'Many other countries haven't either, like the Kenyans. How come a few in a billion people can't...'

'That's true. Indians debate this publicly every four years during the Olympics—when they feel ashamed and humiliated—but outside this window, they forget about it and return to actively discouraging their kids from pursuing careers in sports. In this debate, the reasons offered for India's dismal performance cover the whole gamut: economics, culture, diet, genetics, climate, politics, the dominance of cricket—like soccer in Brazil. A well-known social psychologist has argued that physical competition was never big in India, as it was in Greece and Rome; that the pursuit of sports has been held back due to a very different way of thinking about the self, the individual, and the body. Indians privileged mystical-spiritual pursuits, rather than modern individualism and everything that flows from it—ambition, innovation, competition—helpful for excelling in sports.'

'But Indians *are* ambitious and creative. Look at their magnificent temples and monuments, the sublime art and music, textiles and costumes, cuisines, and on and on.'

'Yes, that requires ambition and creativity. For the

most part though, it wasn't the kind of ambition or creativity that broke away from tradition or community but operated within it, in the service of the social collective—rather than the self, for personal fame and glory, or as physical acts of individual will, which fuel success in modern sports.' He pauses to reflect on his words and soon a debate comes alive in his head. India has counterexamples for nearly everything.

'Interesting theory,' she says thoughtfully. 'Yeah, when it comes down to it, they're such different approaches to life, aren't they? I find India enchanting. Personally, I couldn't care less for modern sports,' she declares. 'I think the West has so much to learn from India. Look where our vain individualism has brought us—colonialism, world wars, WMDs, a culture of violence, drugs, and extreme inequality, environmental and ecological disasters, climate change, factory farming, extinction of species, and on and on. And there is no light at the end of the tunnel, is there?'

He considers standing up for individualism, to cast it in a more balanced light. She is singling out its toxic byproducts—inevitable in a system that inflates egoistic aspirations in men. Doesn't the fiction of individualism also vest certain dignities and rights in individuals that help protect them from the whims of the collective, making room for greater personal development, freedom and justice? But this is a whole different conversation and he postpones it for another time.

Soon they're back on their feet. Their conversation turns to Bay Area hiking spots, packaged food bars, her old car that's falling apart, gossip about friends and colleagues. The lush, fern-lined forest opens into a meadow. The trail continues along a little creek, and across small canyons. They spot black-tailed deer, chipmunks and lizards. By early evening, three hours after starting, they're back in the parking lot. They rest on a stone bench and drink water.

'You know,' she says, 'I love the range of things we can talk about.'

'Me too,' he says. Their eyes meet, they smile. He feels a moment of connection. A surge of affection rises within him. He feels closer to her, more at ease. He wonders what the rest of the evening has in store for them.

§

They reach his place before sundown. He showers before her and starts working on dinner. When she joins him and offers to help, he says, 'Thanks, but it'll be easier if I do the whole thing myself. Perhaps you can pick out a wine and play some music.'

She browses his CDs and picks an album of Romany music that he bought in Budapest years ago. Its vocals have always seemed oddly familiar to him, like echoes from a distant past. She selects an Australian Chablis, pours a glass each, sits at the dining table next to the kitchen, and watches him chop bell peppers and onions, and then fry them with ginger, garlic, mustard, turmeric, coriander and tej patta. 'Mmm, smells delicious,' she says.

She regales him by imitating the accent of a South Indian colleague at work—a sweet man but a total geek, with zero social skills and a seemingly identical roll of the head to indicate both yes and no. But he is such a whiz with databases and networking that their entire office depends on him.

She wanders over to Ved's bookshelves. 'Cute!' she says, picking up the stone figurine of Chac Mool, the Mayan rain god, and comments on some of his other travel souvenirs: the replica of a Sumerian clay tablet; the panpipe from Machu Picchu. He occasionally glances at her from the kitchen, especially when she speaks: 'I never quite figured out Borges'; 'Hemingway is too macho for my taste'; 'Baldwin! I still have a rubbing from his grave. Sorry if this sounds too morbid, but I was really into graves at one time.'

'Can I ask you a question?' she perks up suddenly. 'What would you like to be done to your body after you die? You can take a few minutes to answer it. I'll tell you my answer after yours, okay?'

Ved nods and starts thinking about it. He hears Liz say, 'Gosh, I'm so ignorant about Indian history.' While the curry simmers, he makes rice and a tomato-cucumber raita, and then joins her in the living room.

'You have very few women authors,' her tone carries the whiff of a reprimand.

'Well, women began writing more recently,' he says. 'Men have written more books over time. My collection probably reflects that ratio, especially if you look at older classics.' Even as he says it, it sounds like a flimsy excuse. Really, why hasn't he read more women authors?

'Perhaps men speak to your experiences more than women?'

'That's true to some extent...as much as the reverse is true for you, I guess. But here, let me point out a few women authors from just the top two shelves...Zora Neale Hurston, Sappho, Simone de Beauvoir, Hannah Arendt, Nadine Gordimer, Karen Armstrong.'

'Let's see, that's about 10 per cent. Alright, you get a passing grade. Keep at it though, there's no better way to unlock the feminine mystique.' She looks pleased with her remark.

Favourite authors are next. They both like Mann and Orwell, she likes Atwood and Kundera, he likes Kafka and Milosz. He knows similar tastes in literature do not reflect similar outlooks in life. Much depends on why one likes or dislikes a book. Each person has a unique and autobiographical reading of character and incident. If one probed deep enough, one would find as many responses to the character of Karna as there are readers of the Mahabharata. The devil is always in the details.

'Okay Liz, I have a response to your earlier question. A fitting last rite for my body would be for friends to bury me in an unmarked desert oasis grave, subject to howling winds.'

'Interesting,' she smiles. 'I would like to be buried under a walnut or an oak tree in a generations-old garden, one attached to a house lived in by friends or family.'

'Interesting,' he nods. 'My answer is quite silly actually. What if there is no desert oasis for hundreds of miles around. By the time they find an eligible spot, my body might be smelling pretty bad, and my friends' fondness for me dwindling fast.' She laughs.

'Okay, here is a joke I read today' he says. 'A man writes, "I was so depressed last night thinking about the economy, wars, jobs, my savings, Social Security, retirement funds, etc., I called the Suicide Hotline. I got a call centre in Pakistan, and when they realized I was suicidal, they got all excited, and asked if I could drive a truck."' They laugh together.

He brings out the food to the dining table and they serve themselves.

'Wow, delicious! So full of flavour and body!' she says of his Malabar curry. 'You should write down the recipe.' After dinner, they move to the living room and sit facing each other on the futon. Discussing food, books, and travel, Liz looks relaxed and happy. Her arm rests atop the frame, her reclining posture makes her breasts jut out at him.

'I wish I had met you earlier,' she says. 'You are so different from anyone else I've met. It's amazing how much you've travelled. You should write about your experiences.'

Is she expecting him to make a move, or is that his imagination? He only feels a mild desire to touch her hair, so red and shiny it looks. Before too long he realizes that an hour has gone by since dinner. 'How about some tea?' he asks.

'Great idea. Do you have any decaf or herbal tea?'

'I have mint tea.'

'Perfect.'

He steps into the kitchen. The tension is diffused for a while. She is lying on her tummy on the Moroccan carpet, propped on her elbows over a cushion, her legs folded up and swinging.

Minutes later, he approaches her with two steaming cups of mint tea and a few squares of dark chocolate on a plate. He dims the lights and squats close to her on the carpet.

'Mm … heavenly, thanks.' She takes a few sips, then leans across to reach a lower shelf. Her skirt falls on his outstretched legs. Pulling out a slim volume, she exclaims, 'Gogol! I love Gogol. His stories are so magical. I wish I could write like him.' She stays in that position and in the dim light, reads aloud the blurb on the back cover.

Moved by a nameless urge, he raises his right hand and rubs her back. 'Mm,' She closes her eyes, and leans back, head lowered in repose. His nervousness begins to recede. He moves his hand through her hair, ruffling it, then gently massaging her head. She is enjoying it.

Tick-tock-tick-tock. All at once he is aware of the pendulum clock behind him. He leans forward and gently brushes his nose against hers. 'Traditional Maori greeting,' he whispers.

When he recedes, he notices a beatific smile on her face. 'I hear Maoris are pretty cool people,' she says.

'May I kiss you?' he whispers.

She nods and leans towards him. Their lips meet. Drawing her close, he wraps an arm around her. She reciprocates. They kiss for several minutes; when he makes no additional moves, she nudges his right hand over her breasts. Seconds later they collapse on the Moroccan carpet, grabbing each other awkwardly, tugging at clothes.

They start undressing each other. She is wearing black lace underwear that contrasts with her pale white skin. He wonders if she slipped it on after her shower, expecting this to happen tonight. He likes it when a woman dresses up with sex in mind.

In no time, clothes strewn about, they're naked on his Moroccan carpet. He turns towards her, rolls on top of her and onto the other side. Giggling, she does the same. He repeats. They keep up the rolling game until they reach the kitchen entrance where she ends up on top, squatting on his crotch like an Amazon. Extending his arms, he feels her soft, large bottom.

She is no coy mistress. Lying down next to him, she grabs his right hand and pushes it between her legs. When his fingers hit the mark, she lets out a sharp moan. Her breathing quickens, her fingernails dig into his back as she urgently repeats, 'Gawd, O Gawd.'

Raising herself, she clambers over him, moves up, and straddles his face. Pinned under her bottom, he does the best he can with his tongue. She starts moaning and grinding her pelvis into his face like a possessed woman, nearly smothering him for an instant. An amusing image from long ago crosses his mind, of him stuffing his face into watermelon quarters on sweltering afternoons.

Suddenly a moth appears from nowhere and strikes her face. She jumps, screams, loses her balance, and knocks her forehead against the dining table. The scene changes swiftly. She is on her back, holding her head, sighing in pain, knees bent and held above like an infant's.

He quickly rises, turns up the light and examines the reddish spot on her forehead—a bump is starting to appear. He rushes into the kitchen and returns with a bag of frozen peas wrapped in a kitchen towel.

'Sorry, I hate moths.' She is still searching with fearful eyes, 'Where did it go?'

'Relax, it's gone,' he presses the ice pack on her forehead. 'Why do you hate moths? I think they're cute.'

'Cute? I don't think so. I hate these fat, ugly Bay

Area moths. And cockroaches and mosquitoes.' She looks deadly serious. Her face is contorted with pain. If the moth strikes again, she just might burst into tears, or start screaming.

'Hate is a strong word, my dear. I think the moth just went for the most incandescent thing in the room. But now it has no reason to bother you at all.'

'Very funny,' she lets out a mild chuckle and starts sighing in pain again.

Their interrupted act will have to wait. 'Listen, it's late,' he says. 'And you are in no condition to drive home. Just stay the night.' She agrees without protest.

They retire to his bedroom. Though tired from the hike, his sleep is punctuated by her intermittent moans. He is aware of multiple erections during the night, their hands groping each other in half-sleep. Finally, at four a.m. or so, she manoeuvres herself on top of him. He slips on a condom, she guides him in. She moves with surprising gusto, the bed creaks from their urgent exertions. She turns out to be a screamer.

'Gawd! It has been ages—literally months,' she says right after, recovering her breath. 'How long for you?'

'Too long.'

'No wonder it was quick,' she chuckles. She lies facing him, right leg over his thighs, fingers stroking his chest, 'I like your hairy body. It's so sexy—manly and wild, like an animal.'

'It certainly proves my mammalian credentials,' he says. She chuckles again, then drifts off to sleep and starts snoring. He lies awake pondering her remark and staring at a flickering pattern of light on the ceiling, cast by a defective streetlamp. A thought crosses his mind—could he be content fucking this woman for the rest of his life? Vaguely ashamed for framing it so, he tries to banish the thought. How hushed the city is now, awash in dreams. Finally, dreams overwhelm him too.

§

'Good morning!' he walks in with two cups of coffee on a tray with cookies and turns the Venetian blinds, admitting shafts of sunlight. She sits up against the pillow, squinting her eyes, hair dishevelled, making no attempt to cover her breasts and the loose folds of skin on her midriff.

'The whole block heard your wake-up call this morning,' he teases.

'I bet it was more interesting than a rooster's call.' They laugh. 'Mehdi joked about it too,' she adds. Mehdi, the Egyptian-American doctor and her former boyfriend.

'What was he like?'

'Gosh, looking back, I think he was pretty confused for a forty-year-old. It was as if he was living someone else's script for his life. His attitudes about success and symbols of wealth were so conventional. He also had these weird moods when he'd turn aloof, spacey in fact, when I couldn't fathom him at all. He also umm...resisted public displays of affection, as if he were ashamed even to be seen with me in public. He never introduced me to his friends.'

'The PDA thing was probably cultural,' Ved offers. 'At least in part?'

'I know men and women in Egypt don't touch each other in public. PDA, heaven forbid, would've revealed his sensitive, romantic side—an effeminate trait in his culture. But with him, there was something more. At times, I felt he was punishing me for being white, as if I were a proxy for all the other white women who had spurned him in the past.'

'Hmm. What did you like about him then?'

'Oh, don't get me wrong. He was very decent and kind—he treated me better than any American man has. We shared so many political and social insights. We did volunteer work thrice a week at a free clinic. That was very satisfying. He had lovely, soulful eyes,' she laughs. 'We sure had our moments. He once read me his mother's letters from Cairo. That was so sweet. She sounded wise and wonderful, and so afraid for her son in America. "I know what they think of us," she once wrote to him, "please come back home." That made me all teary.'

Liz continues, 'But then there was that time, I don't remember why, but we were chatting about our sexual fantasies. It came out that incest porn turned him on, as in like father-daughter scenes. That's so spooky in an otherwise decent adult, don't you think?'

'Men have all sorts of spooky fantasies. If ever an evil browser or app secretly tracked and leaked everyone's online porn history, some gobsmacking surprises and reassessments of the human male will surely come out of it. Women will be shocked out of their wits to discover the secret lives of the men in their lives.'

She nods, 'On that note, I have another story, but first let me ask you something. Would you consider a sexual threesome involving another man and your own girlfriend?'

'No. Never felt a desire to do so,' he replies candidly.

'Brownie points for you. My other ex, Peter, said that, if I were agreeable, he'd love to share me with another man, as in a threesome, or just watch me fucking a stranger: voyeurism, you know. The idea turned him on. I kept dismissing it as an idle male fantasy, to be ignored and forgotten. One day it struck me hard that he was so utterly devoid of any sense of possessiveness. That broke something in me, left me cold and sad. I realized—and I am not embarrassed to admit this now—that I want my man to feel a bit territorial over my body, at least enough to not want to share me with others. Peter didn't feel that way. It made me question our entire relationship.'

She leans over to put her coffee cup on the table. He wonders what she would say about him to future lovers. Smart man but too obsessed with ideas? Not vulnerable enough? Too hesitant to let his guard down and get involved with people?

§

Liz takes him to a potluck lunch the following Saturday and introduces him to her friends: a greying novelist and his much younger girlfriend, herself a cookbook author and lingerie model; a high-school teacher; a willowy Salsa dance instructor just back from Cordoba; a college lecturer in women's studies; a currently unemployed graphic designer; and a hippie-ish couple in their mid-thirties, soon to be married in a Buddhist monastery in Thailand.

'It'll be a Buddhist-style marriage ceremony,' the woman clarifies. 'We became Buddhists last year.' She has streaks of blue hair on one side of her head.

So easy to reinvent oneself in this culture, thinks Ved, to get a new faith, persona, identity: the promise of America. He imagines them standing solemnly in a shrine with candles, incense, flowers, and a monk chanting ancient mantras beside a Buddha statue—one set of silly rituals traded for another. But then, whatever floats their boats, he reckons.

He talks to most of them. People discuss recent or upcoming travel, events in the city, foods and recipes. The novelist frets about a bad review of his recent novel in *The Chronicle* and calls the reviewer an oaf; his girlfriend gushes over *Bowling for Columbine*. It strikes Ved that Liz too must share details of her own relationships with some of them, at least going by what she has told him about their relationships. He can feel a few probing eyes: ah-ha, so this is the man Liz is fucking now. A strange phase she is going through, dear woman. Never recovered from Peter, did she?

Beer and wine flow. A large carpet with cushions is spread out in the backyard, where a few of them get stoned and lie in the sun. The graphic designer sings and strums a guitar. The Salsa instructor does a few dance steps, her close-cropped hair accentuating her hoop earrings made by Andean villagers. The high-school teacher, also an active poet in the local scene, reads three new poems linked by a common theme: forgiveness. As a side business, she sells spiritual jewellery, sourced from Dharamshala, India, where she has spent two summers learning to meditate. The university lecturer speaks of her mixed success with growing herbs in her garden. People coalesce in groups, eat and exchange anecdotes from life and work.

On their drive home, Liz asks, 'Did you enjoy it?'

He nods, 'It was alright. Anthropologically interesting.'

She rolls her eyes. 'My friends really liked you.' She offers him snippets of gossip about some of them. Then she asks, 'Amanda is hosting a party at her place in two weeks. She told me she would love to have you over. Would you like to join me?'

'That's the college lecturer?'

'Yes.'

'I'll pass.'

'Ah, so you didn't like them.'

'It's not that. It's just that I have no great desire to spend more time with them.'

'But they're my friends,' she asserts. 'They are very genuine people, and interesting too—it takes time to get to know people.'

'Yes, I'm sure, but they didn't strike me as all that interesting. I'd rather read a book.'

'Don't trash my friends!' she snaps. 'I sometimes forget that you are the only interesting person left in the world.'

'I'm not trashing anyone. It's just that I'm not looking for a new circle of friends right now, or to merely hang out with people. I first wrote to you because you interested me. I didn't think it would automatically mean attending your friends' parties too.'

'Okay, okay, I get it!' she raises her voice in exasperation. 'Fine, I won't invite you to hang out with them ever again. I'm sure they will get over their terrible loss.' She starts to sulk.

He regrets his bluntness. What's the matter with him?

Are kindness and empathy mere abstract ideas to him? Not hitting it off with her friends is no good reason to be so dismissive of them. He slips into a daydream: He runs into himself in a park, an encounter with his exact copy. He is horrified; he does not enjoy meeting himself. End of daydream.

She resumes, 'But I would still like to meet your friends, and I'm not averse to getting to know them better.'

He quickly backpedals, 'I'm sorry but I'm not much of a partygoer...I don't make friends easily...I'm trying to simplify my life,' all of which have elements of truth. That's just his temperament, he wants to say. He can't become a different person now, at least not for long. She continues to sulk until they get to her place and have makeup sex.

§

They start meeting on weekends, alternating between their apartments. On her second visit, she complained of stale odours in his towels and bed linen. 'I'm sorry, but I have a very keen sense of smell,' she explained. So each time before her arrival, he replaces the sheets and towels. With her around, he bathes twice a day, lest he reinforce any lingering stereotypes of the smelly-oily Indian male in her mind.

'I wish we lived closer,' she said, 'so we could also meet during the week.' Her place in Marin is about an hour away.

'Yeah, but our current arrangement has its own advantages. Don't you think it fosters a sense of longing for the weekend and makes the time we spend together more fun?'

She looks sceptical. 'If that is so, why can't you at least call during the week?'

They see indie films on weekends, go on hikes, and while away afternoons on the lush lawns of her local park. They discuss books and movies. She plays the piano at times. He envies how she loses herself in her music, slipping into another world, without a trace of self-consciousness. She has a weakness for dark chocolates and ice cream. She was overjoyed both times he arrived at her place with a pint of chocolate gelato.

He likes the well-kept yard behind her building, with plum, orange, apricot and lemon trees. She dries her laundry in the sun, on a clothesline in her balcony. Once he saw her fraying lace panties flutter in the breeze alongside her neighbour's US flag. He was amused by the sight and thought that it would make an interesting arty photograph.

But the flag by itself is not amusing. Flags in America make him anxious, and, of late, they are everywhere: on jacket lapels, cars, shop fronts, windows, roofs. Patriotism, he has long held, is the yoke of the simpleton and 'the last refuge of the scoundrel'. It provokes a long-submerged dread in him. In an old anxiety dream of his, a cute little girl with golden curls waving a paper flag walks up to him and says, 'Hey mister, go home!' It hasn't actually happened yet.

Though he considers their sex life satisfying enough, he finds himself initiating sex less and less often. Half the time he does it from a sense of expectation. She has also shown him her battery-operated dildo, a birthday gift from a girlfriend. It replaced a plain silicone one she had, a part of which—she revealed this with embarrassed laughter—accidentally melted while she was disinfecting it in boiling water. When he cajoled her, she agreed with a laugh, 'Fine, someday when I am in the mood, I'll give you a live demo. Men are so weird this way!'

He learns that her grasp of numbers is feeble at best—she uses millions, billions and trillions as qualitative descriptors. Her estimate of the GDP of the US was off by two orders of magnitude. He notices an empty case of Prozac capsules in her bathroom trash bin. He decides he will not ask her about it unless she brings it up herself, someday.

He discovers more of her pet peeves: the menace of cloning and designer babies, GMOs, Internet porn, SUV owners, the Christian Coalition, the gun lobby. Bumper stickers on her aging Honda Civic include A WOMAN'S PLACE IS IN THE HOUSE AND THE SENATE; THE PATRIOT ACT IS UN-PATRIOTIC; and LIVE SIMPLY THAT OTHERS MAY SIMPLY LIVE.

Their spirited debates continue as before. One time she set off on the youth-obsessed American culture and the skinny ideals of female beauty manufactured by the consumer industry—a conspiracy, she said, to keep women down.

'But women don't have to buy into those ideals,' he said.

That set her off. 'Spoken like a man! You don't know the pressure this culture puts on women, how it ruins their self-esteem, causes them anxiety and self-loathing, not to mention eating disorders and health problems. Many college sororities even have puking contests after dinner. You don't know because you are not constantly evaluated by the shape of your tits and butt, are you? What pains me more is the knowledge that so many women don't see the big picture and become co-conspirators with men in their own oppression.'

Ved lets it go, remembering the painful experiences that surely made this topic very personal—her ex, Peter, had left her for a younger skinny blonde. She is quite right too. Indeed, Ved thinks, how well does he really understand the social experience of women? Isn't he himself part of the problem when he gravitates towards these narrow ideals of female beauty?

Another day, she complained bitterly that the American news media is the most biased and jingoistic in the world and censors so much about US foreign policy. Look at how so many news organizations helped buttress the case for the Iraq war. 'If only Americans were given the whole truth, they would do the right thing more often.'

'I'm not so sure,' he responded. 'I don't think most Americans want to hear the whole truth about America's foreign policy. Humans everywhere don't like to hear disturbing truths of any kind. They deny or avoid the whole truth because they can't handle it. How many seek out such truths on "alternative" media? Combine this inclination with the free market, and what you inevitably get is news that sells like any consumable, made palatable, affirming the myth of national greatness and benevolence, all while serving the interests of the powerful.'

'Yes, that's more or less what Chomsky says. But

remember Vietnam? Millions of Americans responded when they discovered the truth.'

'Did they respond to the truth, or to the draft and the body bags coming home?'

'Fair point. This is hard for me to accept sometimes. Yes, as long as minorities and poor soldiers do the dying—but not in large numbers and without graphic images of their suffering—most Americans will not question what their leaders do abroad. Blimey! as they say in England, now we even have ultra-hi-tech weapons to minimize American casualties in war. To make things worse, Americans are big-time into patriotism. It gives me the creeps to see all those Bible-thumping, flag-waving, gun-toting, xenophobic patriots of Middle America.'

She continues, 'It's true most Americans don't care enough, and corporate media panders to their basest instincts for the sake of profit.' She throws her hands up in the air. 'They're too busy making mind-numbing soaps, sitcoms, sensational stories and gossip—rather than honest reportage. They indulge in fear mongering because it's profitable. Where will all this lead us?'

'Why, to your giant ball of fire of course,' he quipped. 'The end times are nigh! Get ready for the Rapture! Or more likely, since you haven't fully surrendered your heart to Jesus, get ready for the Tribulation! During the seven-year pestilence, the Antichrist...'

'Stop! That's a very charming image but I get the drift,' she is amused.

'Well,' he said, turning pensive, 'I think apathy to truth is not just an American problem. It is universal. But the thing is that the whole world suffers more from apathy to the truth in the US, as opposed to say in Bolivia, because the US is so much more powerful. Our best hope lies in enough citizens being vigilant against wilful abuses of power and trust. Basic decency and an informed citizenry are both required for democracy to work. I mean, with too many dumbass citizens, democracy too can produce horrific outcomes.'

'Exactly. And we're so cocky about spreading so-called democracy around the world, when our own is so fragile and can be so easily manipulated and gutted. Look at this joke of a president!'

'Yes, making democracy work is a continual, uphill struggle against illiberal forces that seem more elemental, ruthless, determined. What happened to ancient Athens can well happen again today. I sometimes think democracy, especially one that emphasizes rights far more than responsibilities, sows the seeds of its own destruction. The jury is still out on this modern experiment of ours, isn't it?'

His words darkened her mood, stoked her pessimism. She began ranting again: 'It's not like we don't have enough problems already! American politicians and corporate globalization have turned our system into an oligarchy and raised the stakes for the entire planet. It's such a terrible time to be American. Makes me want to puke, and move to Canada. The only problem is,' she sat shaking her head,. 'it's too damn cold up there!'

§

Ravi calls one morning, 'I'm back and I'm a married man!'

Ved meets him for lunch in the cafeteria. 'You look tired,' Ved says with a wink. 'Not getting enough sleep?'

'Ha, ha. It's not what you think. It's the jetlag.'

Ravi shares the essential details. Kavita was the third woman he met and he liked her instantly. They decided to tie the knot after two long dinner dates. They got married six days before the return flight, at an hour appointed by their family's astrologer.

'Man, during those never-ending ceremonies and photo sessions, I had to keep a smile on for so long that my face hurt when it went back to normal,' he chuckles.

Luckily, Kavita already had a multiple-entry tourist visa from a previous visit to the US; she'll now seek another visa for her new status. They stopped for a long weekend in Singapore, a honeymoon of sorts, away at last from what he called their 'hordes of pesky relatives.'

So that's where they first had sex, thinks Ved, in a Singapore high-rise hotel overlooking the sea. Her clammy, hennaed hands and feet wrapped around his heaving body; her twinge of pain, virgin blood on the sheets—and a satisfied smile on Ravi's face.

Ravi shows him pictures of Kavita, whom Ved finds conventionally attractive. 'She has an aunt in Jersey City and college friends in many states, so the culture shock should be mild,' says Ravi. She already has her favourite TV shows, Hollywood and MTV stars, cosmetics, and clothing brands. Her software experience should make it easier for her to get a job.

How times have changed, thinks Ved. Unlike today's kids from Indian metros, the US was so much more daunting to him. He grew up with almost no exposure to American TV or Hollywood. His parents first got a TV in the early eighties, when he was in his mid-teens. The first time he used a Western-style toilet was at the age of sixteen. Pizza and burgers were unfamiliar foods. He came to the US a virgin. In his early days in the US, soda vending machines, checkout counters, ATMs and gas station stores were utter novelties to him. It was perhaps this experience that had sensitized him to the experience of provincials in a metropolis, especially those consigned to the margins for their strange manners and customs. He thinks Czesław Miłosz captured this beautifully in his poem, 'Youth'.

'How are things going between you two?' Ved asks.

'Fine,' says Ravi, 'We're getting to know each other. I've had to recalibrate myself a little because she comes from a very protective background. She is shy and homesick. She cries often and calls her mother every day.'

Ravi pauses, scratches his head and resumes, 'You know how Indian girls are, a bit too conservative. "Arrey!" I teased her, "Your sexual hang-ups are unworthy of a culture that gave Kama Sutra to the world."' He laughs, waving his hand nonchalantly, 'But that's no big deal. I will teach her in due course.'

'She'll be fine. Be patient and sensitive,' offers Ved, wondering how Ravi's unrequited lust for white chicks would manifest itself in this union. Wasn't Kavita a sexual compromise in his mind long before he even met her? Poor thing, to have him for her sex teacher. What cocktail of female insecurities lies ahead in her American life?

§

'Would you like to take our relationship to the next stage?' Liz asks at the end of their seventh weekend together.

'What next stage?'

'Where we are officially an item, where we can say, "Hey, meet my significant other". Where we would plan vacations, have keys to each other's apartments, meet each other's friends, and so on. When we would even consider cohabitating.'

He had seen this coming. He knew that after the initial rush, the novelty and the sex, will come expectations, obligations. Yet he's amazed by the clarity of the next stage in her mind. No, he does not want her next stage. Best to be honest, he tells himself. Best to avoid games for his own sake, for his own peace of mind. But how exactly should he convey this?

'I'll be honest with you Liz,' he says pensively, 'I enjoy your company very much, and I learn from you. I think you are a terrific person, smart and intelligent.'

'That's how I feel about you too.' She has an anxious look.

'But I doubt—I'm not sure if we can be soulmates to each other in the usual sense.' He looks straight into her eyes, 'I feel there is something missing right now, some ingredient that I cannot pinpoint exactly.' Something, it's clear to him, that goes well beyond his lukewarm physical attraction to her.

She doesn't look surprised. In fact, she does not betray any emotion at all.

'I do enjoy your company, I'm sure you can tell,' he adds. 'So let me ask you instead. Can we be together knowing that our relationship, like most others these days, will have a finite life: a beginning, middle, and end? Let's not even pretend otherwise, or try to consign it to some official relationship category.

'In other words,' he continues, 'however long we are together, possibly a long time, would be our sole and mutual reward. It would be our enlightened statement to the world: I am with my lover because I simply enjoy being with my lover, and do not care for the trappings of traditional unions.'

'Hmm, why am I not surprised to hear that?' she sounds hurt.

'Well, what do you think?

'It's late now. I'll have to think about it.'

When he leaves a few minutes later, Liz seems withdrawn, which worries him. For all he knows, it might soon be over between them. She did make it clear upfront that she was looking for something much more solid. He gives their imminent breakup more than an even chance.

Driving home, his mind is a jumble of emotions. So painful, this never-ending wear and tear on the soul. Who can take such relationship turmoil for the rest of his life? Yet, isn't it true that Liz wasn't right for him? Is there any woman, anywhere, who is right for him? he despairs.

On the highway, his thoughts drift to Sasha. She had emailed him three days earlier from a beach resort in Costa Rica, where she is on vacation with the salesman Ved had driven her to see at the Plaza Hotel. She mentioned a white sand beach, coconutty cocktails and visiting a volcano. He hopes the salesman is treating her right, and that she struck a good deal to grant certain rights to her body for a whole week, 24/7.

Nine

RETURNING HOME ON SUNDAY NIGHT, he finds a voicemail from Ravi, 'Hey man, guess what? A huge layoff is hitting Omnicon tomorrow. Call me ASAP.'

'How do you know?' Ved calls him back.

'From my friend Vivek in Finance. He's an insider but he told me on the condition that I don't tell anyone else—I'm only telling you. Please keep it to yourself.'

'Sure. Did he say what projects or divisions?'

'Across the board,' Ravi says. 'He thinks the cut may be as high as 20 per cent. Jesus fuckin' Christ! I'm shitting bricks man. I'm on my third gin and tonic.'

'Save the gin and tonic. We might need some tomorrow night.'

Ravi laughs, 'And what perfect timing! The market is in a tailspin again, people acting like sheep and dumping Omnicon stock en masse, driving our net worth into the ground. Fuckin' lemmings, man! How much lower can the NASDAQ go?'

'A lot. The last time I checked it was well above zero.'

Nervous titters follow. Seems like only yesterday when those who were not playing the stock market were deemed either daft or cowardly by the rest. Cab drivers fished for stock tips. An Indian restaurateur in San Mateo told Ved that his astrologer not only gave him stock tips but also revealed the auspicious hour to buy them. The latest get-rich-quick scheme in town had been to get a desk job in a hi-tech startup. Even secretaries were said to have become millionaires overnight. A psychosis had overtaken the media and the markets. In this 'new economy', revenue was deemed too old-fashioned and unnecessary for success. Startups received tens of millions of dollars in funding without a business plan. Many even went public with absurd valuations.

Then came the economic tailspin. The dotcom bubble burst; tech companies imploded, creating jobless hordes. Many stocks lost over 98 per cent of their peak values. Ingenious stock-trading malpractices and corporate crimes came to light. Consumer confidence collapsed. Some had said this was a healthy correction, after which the markets would rise again. So much in daily life, Ved reflects with disquiet, has come to depend on the markets rising and rising and rising.

§

Monday morning, Ved finds a hush has befallen his office. Multiple notices announce a mandatory all-hands briefing at two p.m. His desk looks normal—no yellow notes stuck to the monitor, no voicemail, even his network password still works. Ved talks to his neighbour in business development, the one with the partner-or-perish mantra. He is quietly ecstatic, having beaten his own odds of surviving. Leaning closer, he whispers the names of a few colleagues laid-off this morning, 'If your network password works, rejoice!'

Ved breathes a sigh of relief.

He notices Sally, a hardware program manager, weeping in her cubicle as she talks on the phone. Sally had a particularly good time at Omnicon's holiday party last December. She got swept up by the convivial bonhomie of the hour, the lavish meal, gifts exchanged by lots. She was among the people dancing to and screaming out the lyrics of 'Born to be Wild'. Ved recalls being tickled by the thought that they would all be back in their cubicles on Monday in business-casual attires to pore over staid presentations, emails and spreadsheets.

The story going around is that a power struggle between the hardware and software camps degenerated into name calling at a board meeting last month. The hardware camp lost out. Omnicon, as many Wall Street analysts had urged, is scaling down its ailing hardware business. The timing was deemed convenient for a bit of pruning in other divisions too. Altogether, 10,000 people have been laid-off worldwide, with many locations entirely shut down—a major surgical job. Besides all this, an earnings warning has been issued for the year ahead.

Ravi calls, 'Game over man. The bastards axed me too.' His voice is charged and hurt. 'They just kicked me out with all my personal stuff. Three years of my life here man, and they treated me like a fuckin' Untouchable!'

Ved goes down to meet him in the parking lot, 'Ouch, I am sorry man.' Ravi shrugs, shaking his head. He looks shocked.

'Fucked up timing, man. I'm in deep shit.' He had just weeks to go before he got his Green Card, which he had applied for three years earlier. Now he has thirty days to find another job or return to India, or become illegal. Ved wonders what his new wife might think about all this.

Ravi describes how it happened. When he came in, an admin asked him to immediately see John, his VP. Ravi's heart had missed a beat; he knew the reason at once. His mind racing, and a visibly impatient admin tagging behind, he stopped in the kitchen to brew his customary cup of morning tea—his last one at Omnicon—before stepping into John's office. A woman from Human Resources was also present to perform what Ravi called 'the last rites'.

'We have come to a parting of ways...' John gave him the official talk about hard times and the difficult choices they were forced to make. The meeting lasted ten minutes. John was trying so hard to appear fair and sensitive that it felt like a staged performance. 'Imagine my misery,' he said, 'to be given this horrible job of letting people go.'

John expressed sympathy for the crisis this 'unfortunate separation' poses for Ravi's immigration status. He asked the HR woman to explore possible options, but she apologized with a straight face, adding that they can't bend any rules. 'I am sure it was an act,' says Ravi, 'so the bastard would come across as a good guy. It was very much a good cop–bad cop routine.'

The HR woman gave him a checklist of formalities to complete. His network password was disabled already. Too shocked to say goodbye to anyone, he began gathering his personal items into two cardboard boxes. Just as Ravi was about to make a copy of his personal data on his laptop—his emails, documents, music, images—the HR woman arrived. 'No,' she said bluntly, 'that's not allowed; everything on this computer legally belongs to Omnicon.'

machines with virtualized intrusion traps (DIMVITs) are transforming lives. Many other portfolios are strong. I have no doubt that Omnicon will rebound and again become the darling of Wall Street.'

Towards the end, Greg turns melancholy, 'We live in hard times, in a world going crazy with war, fear and uncertainty. The only takeaway nugget of wisdom I can offer is something very simple: Be human. Yes, be human first, before being an employee.'

The crowd responds with a hearty applause, a colleague next to Ved sneaks a tissue up to her eyes. A splendid performance, Ved thinks, worthy of a shrewd leader. The kind Ved knows he himself will never be, beset as he is with too much doubt and brooding—and not enough killer instinct and decisiveness, or unctuousness for that matter. As in religion and politics, people also want business leaders who display an aura of strength and command, empathy and optimism. He is glad he did not join the knee-jerk applause for Greg.

§

All of Monday, the global media is awash with the news from Omnicon. Ved's parents call and worriedly ask about his job. 'I knew it!' Mother exclaims, voice bubbling with pride. 'I told your father they don't fire intelligent people.'

'Ma, nobody got fired. This was a layoff—a reduction in force.' There, he is using that euphemism himself. Before too long he will be using 'collateral damage' in casual conversation. 'Some projects were dropped for business reasons. It had little to do with my intelligence.'

She remains sceptical. In her world, a stigma surrounds

anyone who loses a job, and it must somehow relate to the employee's intellect or conduct.

Their visit is only three weeks away and they sound excited. They're shopping for things they imagine he misses in America. 'Just bring yourselves. I get everything here now. You'll be amazed.' Since their last visit, many more Indian software engineers had come to fuel the Silicon Valley boom of the late nineties. Along with them came the trappings a wealthy diaspora needs to feel at home: desi grocery stores, restaurants, movie theatres, temples, dating clubs and more.

He boils a pack of frozen spinach tortellini for dinner and adds a garlic-basil pasta sauce, pickled olives, and garam masala. At bedtime, he hears a bed creaking in the apartment above. A young couple has recently moved in. The round-faced woman with perky breasts and tattoos on both arms is from Orange County and came to introduce herself the other day. He has seen her man too: tall, muscular and full of youthful swagger. Now the two are fucking their brains out.

He starts to masturbate on his bed, placed directly beneath theirs. Eerie, he thinks. How many eons of nature's toil fashion these silly acts? The creaking gets more frantic. Through the wood ceiling, he can hear her muffled cries of 'harder, sweetie, harder'. Her final orgasmic cry echoes in his mind long after, as he lies face down, spent, thinking how much of his life is dream and appetite, punctuated by moments of alertness.

Ved suddenly bursts out laughing. What if he had a fatal cardiac arrest while masturbating? They would find him in this state: hand on dick, cotton rag beneath.

They would snap pictures of him in that state. Super embarrassing. But he would be dead, right? Part of the great oblivion. Why does it bother him what people might think of him after his death?

§

Ravi calls the next day, 'I blew it man, blew it.'

'What are you talking about?'

'Randy called, Omnicon's Director of HR. The bastard. He started off real friendly, with this fake intimate tone. He tells me he "regrets" that my final interaction with his colleague was "less than cordial". And that he "cares deeply" about this stuff—about how people experience their workplaces and some bullshit about "dignity" and "human capital." I was totally fuckin' spooked! Then he got to the point.'

Randy said that network monitoring and file-system analysis of Ravi's computer had revealed that someone had used it repeatedly to access and download pornographic content, violating Omnicon's corporate policies. 'In light of my long and unique contributions, the fucker said, he had decided to call and alert me to this finding,' Ravi said.

'Why?' Ved asks.

'Because the HR female who escorted me out had told Randy about my threat to sue Omnicon. He was calling to warn me against it,' Ravi fumed. 'He mentioned that Omnicon's lawyers might need to cite their findings in court if forced to defend Omnicon against an unfair dismissal allegation. Under California law, he said, such findings are adequate grounds for dismissal.'

Ravi continued, 'I was totally stunned, man. My

lawsuit idea went up in smoke. Then suddenly Randy softens up and says, "Hey, man, I get it that some of these policies are pretty hard-ass. I get that what we call a "violation" is just a harmless diversion—we're all grown-ups here, aren't we? So why don't we resolve this matter the way grown-up men ought to, as a win-win?" Then the madarchod says he has a solution I would "surely appreciate".'

Randy offered an additional two months of severance pay to Ravi. In return, Ravi would simply need to sign a release form stating that he won't litigate against Omnicon. Randy has put the form in the mail already. The offer is valid for a week.

'So what do you think?' Ved asks.

'Fuckin' savages, man!'

Ten

VED AND LIZ ATTEND A house concert that she had booked weeks ago in her neighbourhood. A trio plays traditional folk songs from Greece, Turkey and Bulgaria. Afterwards, though still early for dinner, they walk to an Italian restaurant. Liz looks a bit aloof and distracted.

'Amazing performance!' Ved says. 'It made me imagine a bygone era of music: travelling bands, uncluttered sound, simple instruments, songs rooted in place.' Liz agrees with a feeble smile. Once they settle down, he asks, 'What's on your mind, Liz?'

'You know what's on my mind.'

'Well then, let's talk about it?'

She sighs deeply. 'Ved, about your offer last Sunday, I am sorry but it seems like a classic hedge to me. You want to keep a foot out the door.'

'I'm sorry you see it that way. I see it as living each day as it comes, in tune with the impermanence of the universe. Let me ask you, Liz, is it not more reasonable to be with someone based on the principle of…'

'Sweetheart,' she cuts him off sharply, 'I'm not looking for some "reasonable deal," nor an arrangement based on dry principles—your principles. I don't want this to be on your terms entirely. What about what I want?'

He is floored by the intensity of her response. 'Well, tell me. What do you want?'

'To be loved, to be in love. I want my partner and me to be significant anchors and a daily presence in each other's lives. I want to grow old with him. I said that even before we met. Otherwise, what's the point? I might as well be alone.'

'In other words, you prefer the rent-to-own model to the lease-as-you-please model.'

'This is no time for flippancy, Ved. We are not discussing furniture for god's sake. But if you must put it that way, the answer is...yes. Unlike you, I neither wish to make any societal statements nor forsake the "trappings of traditional unions".'

'You want commitment, assurances, a roadmap for the relationship?'

'Yes. At this point in my life, I deserve it. I got burned with Peter. I lived by his terms and ended up with nothing. I don't want to repeat that mistake. I'm in no hurry to work out every detail upfront, but I want my life-partner to take a leap of faith with me, one that seeks to erase borders between us. I don't get the sense you are ready for it. Are you? Please be honest, Ved.'

He does not like this talk. 'True. I'm not ready for leaps of faith, or erasing borders.'

She stares out the window for a few seconds, then says in a sad, hurtful voice, 'I am not surprised you say that. You probably don't even know what it means. That's because, like most men, you are not in touch with your feelings.'

The rebuke annoys him but he tries not to show it.

'Thanks for the insight, but I know my feelings well enough. If men and women differ, it may be because they have different problem-solving techniques—the problem of being in the world—and which likely has its roots in the Pleistocene—'

'That may be true in conceptual terms,' she cuts him off, 'something you have a special flair for, but you really need to look within yourself, Ved. You're so much like a fortress. You don't reveal your heart to anyone. You don't make yourself vulnerable, show no weaknesses. Do you ever cry? You've got this...this hard shell around you that shuts out everyone else. You don't surrender your—'

'I don't need a lecture on my deficiencies.'

But there is no stopping her. 'You just love your high perch, don't you?' She says 'love' mockingly. 'From up there, you observe and study your fellow humans, who invariably fail to live up to your standards. You don't ever reveal your worries, Ved. I don't mean your worries about the fate of humanity, which you talk plenty about, but private worries, related to your life. You surely have some, I know you do.'

'I don't like to burden others with my little worries. That's just my nature.'

'You don't get it, do you? What if your life partner joyfully wants to share your burden? The way you are,' she shakes her head in exasperation, 'how can you ever fall in love? Do you even recognize the feeling of being in love? Love, this all-encompassing—'

'Stop it! We all have different ways of feeling and expressing love. I have my own.'

'But in my experience, I find you stingy with love

and affection. You are obsessed with being measured and reasonable, too stoic, suspicious of your feelings and emotions. You expect others to live up to your standards, or you withhold your respect and write them off as people unworthy of—'

'Shhh!' he raises a finger to his lips. 'Lower your voice, this is a public place.'

'I don't care Ved,' her voice is loud as ever. 'The truth is that in our relationship—you might as well know this, it might help you in the future—I often feel like I am not quite real in your mind, rather a curiosity, a human specimen, to be studied and managed. I think you're a smart and decent man, but you're cold and aloof. Women are not endeared by such qualities.'

He feels the urge to bluntly point out that perhaps what gets in the way of warmth is all her ranting, her million resentments at the world. He too is not endeared by the mushy, carping quality of her complaints at the world, which spill over to impair her capacity for joy and serenity. And what's up with that soppy spirituality, the fake nobility she sees in tradition, the reverence for ancient wisdom? She is a Luddite at heart. But he does not say it. Confronting her now with her own flaws would be messy and unkind. He lets her talk and responds only in brief, general terms. Dinner is marked by long silences. They eat little.

After he settles the bill, they walk back to her place. 'Let me ask you something, Ved. About that leap of faith I mentioned, is it just me you're not prepared to make that leap with? Please be honest.'

Not a question he wants to answer but he finds

himself saying, 'Well, I think that is partly true, yes. The other, bigger part is more complex. Perhaps I am just not ready to make a leap of faith—with anyone.'

She bursts into tears on the poorly lit sidewalk. They arrive at her apartment complex. She slumps heavily on the staircase to her floor. Across the parking lot, a family of raccoons forages the trash bins. He hears a distant ambulance, a night of emergency for someone.

She sobs into a napkin and speaks in fits and starts, 'Why is life so awful? I'm almost forty-one, stuck in a low-wage job. I still have debts, a mother showing signs of Alzheimer's. I'm no longer young or beautiful...and I won't look even half as good in a few years. If I don't find a man soon, I never will. Why is it so hard for me? I had such high hopes this time.'

He struggles to figure out what to say. He moves closer and sits next to her. Her sobbing has nearly stopped. 'I'm sorry it didn't work out, Liz. I'm sorry for disappointing you. I began with an open mind. But better now than later, when the pain and disruption would've been more. Along the way, I hope we both learned a few things about ourselves. I know I did.'

'I wish I could say that,' her tone is full of bitter disdain. Save for the faint roar of the highway, it is very quiet.

So this is it, the end of their relationship. What more is left to be said? He rises and stands facing her in an implicit gesture of leave-taking. She, too, knows that the moment has come, and rises to give him a final hug.

Against his better instincts, he says, 'Let's keep in touch. We have so much in common.'

'That rarely works out, but we can try.' Is that a faint smile, or is she about to cry again?

Before turning away, he looks at her: a thickset middle-aged woman, soulful and intelligent, who briefly came into his life, now slumped on the stairs of an apartment complex, swaddled in ill-fitting clothes, puffy eyes, sticky hair, crumpled napkin in hand, feeling sorry for herself and angry at him. He feels sorry for her too. He knows this image will stay with him for a long time. Her mood rubs off on him. Walking to his car, he too is depressed, drained to the core.

It was an enriching affair, for sure. But didn't he suspect there was no future in it from the moment he first saw her over two months ago? That's how it turned out, and now he is back to square one. Like soft rolling thunder, the dread of loneliness courses through him.

Why do her words rankle so much? They feel like a judgment and a sentence combined: thou art too guarded, aloof, stingy with love, miserly with affection, not vulnerable, lacking in warmth, with walls around to exclude others from thine inner sanctum.

Pooja too, he suspects, would have agreed. Though raised in the US, she was close enough to Indian culture to know him in ways Liz never could. In fact, Liz was in love with an idea of India that he could barely relate to. It would've been hard for Liz to understand so much that was a part of him, without his choosing—how his old-world culture had shaped his tastes, habits, and sense of displacement. What Liz had to offer was different and not quite enough.

His mind swims. If shared culture is so strong a force,

what does it mean to be a citizen of the world? If he could imagine a perfect woman with the skill of a literary master and breathe life into her, would they have a perfect relationship? He doubts it. There is still so much within him to prevent that from happening—his own ghosts that he does not yet well understand.

§

Sasha calls on Saturday evening. 'Hi, I am ten minutes away and can stop by.'

'Come on over! I'll make some tea.'

His spirits lift on seeing her. She looks relaxed and cheerful, and even has a moderate suntan. 'Is that new?' he asks, pointing to her long suede jacket.

'Yes, a gift from George,' her companion in Costa Rica, whose lust she first slaked nearly three months ago while he waited outside the Plaza Hotel. Underneath her jacket is a pink spandex camisole and matching hot pants. Her smooth legs disappear inside shiny black boots.

She sits at the dining table while he makes tea, 'So what is he like, this fellow George?'

'A nice man, always talking and making jokes, though I don't get many of them and he has to explain.' After that first time, George saw her once every few weeks, whenever he visited San Francisco. One day he suggested Costa Rica. 'He was married once and lived in Cincinnati. He said his wife divorced him after she caught him with her younger sister. That was two years ago. He then moved from Cincinnati to Boston, where he grew up. He is like a company man, not thinking man like you. He is very fond of American football.'

'Why isn't he dating anyone now?' Ved asks.

'He finds American women too high maintenance. "I am done with them," he said.'

Is he among those white men who chase Eastern women for all the wrong reasons? Ved wonders. But then, how many men and women anywhere chase each other for the right reasons?

Over tea, she talks about the resort, local sightseeing and impressions of Costa Rica. 'Now he wants me to visit him in Boston next month. He'll send me a ticket.'

'Wow, looks like our man is quite taken in with your Ruski magic,' he jokes.

Without warning, she lowers her camisole to expose a breast, 'You want Ruski magic?'

A windfall, he thinks. 'Show me!' Before she can change her mind, he takes her hand and leads her to the bedroom. Seconds later, they are beneath the sheets, naked.

She likes the Indian classical flute and guitar music that he has put on. While he delights in her body—her soft skin, hair, breasts—she lies there mesmerized by the music, with no evident interest in sex, yet yielding to his roving hands, as if by reflex. She emerges from her musical reverie, they have sex. She offers to rub his back the way he likes it, he readily accepts.

'I really thought you found a girlfriend and will not see me again,' she says afterwards.

'I told you about the product launch. It is now finished, in fact, finished last weekend,' he smiles. 'So what brought you to my neighbourhood?'

She reveals that it was a dry call—the client didn't

even touch her. He asked her to remove her shorts, recline on a sofa, close her eyes, and play with herself, while he jacked-off a few feet away. He paid for an hour but sent her away in thirty minutes.

Since the dotcom bust, Sasha says, her business has slowed. Earlier, during the glory days of venture capital and IPOs, the oldest profession got cozy with the newest. Flush with their millions, geeks who couldn't even get a date hired the services of porn stars. Baby-faced CEOs frequented dominatrixes. A few celebrated their IPOs in Las Vegas brothels. Not as many men call her now, says Sasha, and their sessions are shorter. There is a glut of escort girls, competition is intense. The girls have to do more to get repeat business.

'How far I have come from home! What a world I live in,' she turns pensive. 'I never thought I will do this work. I want to be an artist. When I think of my dead mother watching from above, I am filled with shame.'

This is the first time she has said this to him, he thinks. 'No reason for shame,' he adds, then immediately regrets its glibness: what does he know of the indignity she feels in submitting her body to the prying hands of strange men?

'I don't like this work, but to get a job in America I need a work permit or a Green Card.'

They've talked about this before. He can't really help her, except introduce her to a good immigration lawyer, which he did months ago. She must find someone to sponsor her for another visa: an employer, a close blood relative, or a husband. Or she must leave the country.

'Next weekend my parents are arriving from India

for two months,' he tells her when she is putting on her boots. 'I'll be busy with them. But maybe we can meet for lunch some time.'

'Lucky you! Enjoy your time with them.' She gives him a hug and leaves. He steps out on his balcony and watches her emerge from the flight of steps onto the street, and then beyond till she turns the corner. Twilight hour. Amid the sounds of city life, he is calm and happy. He can feel his heart brimming with a nameless gratitude.

Eleven

How his father has aged since Ved saw him eighteen months ago. He looks frail and deflated. Despite his afternoon siesta, he dozes off at odd hours, while watching the news on TV, even in the front seat of the car. He and Mother arrived three weeks ago, so jet lag can be ruled out. His facial skin has grown even more leathery and loose, accentuating the deep-set eyes on his long face. The few tufts of grey hair above his earlobes have shrunk further.

Of the two of them, Mother has aged better. Short and thin, she is four years younger and has fewer wrinkles for her age. Even her eyes seem more alert than Father's. Her hair, which she dyes with henna, gives her a more youthful appearance.

This is their second visit to America but the first one to his apartment in San Francisco. A day after their arrival, Ved gave them a walking tour of his neighbourhood, around shops and restaurants, a park and the public library. Twice a day now, they venture out for walks on their own. He worries about them while he's at work. Much can go wrong with elderly foreigners in a big city. They too would amplify every negative encounter, as novice travellers are wont to. He has given them a mobile phone, calls often to check up on them, and tries to leave work early.

The first few days, whenever they noticed trash by the roadside, they would exclaim, 'Arrey, look! Just like India!' Clear evidence that streets in their own country aren't as uniquely trash-ridden as so many spitefully accuse them of being. During her last visit, Mother had felt a bit self-conscious wearing her sari, but now she seems more at ease in it. Each time they go out, she spots a few other sari-clad mothers visiting their offspring in America. As on their last visit, they find it odd that total strangers smile at them on the streets. As always, they speak to each other in Hinglish.

By now, their routines have settled down exactly as Ved had expected. They rise well before him each morning. Mother has taken over the kitchen and learned to operate most of his appliances. She starts each day with a quick puja before a cheap portrait of Ganesh that he had picked up for her at an Indian store. By breakfast time, the living room is suffused with the aroma of fresh spices. He protests often, 'Ma, you need to cut down on kitchen work and enjoy your vacation,' but his words fall on deaf ears. She is determined to cook all of his favourite foods during her stay.

'While I'm here, there will be only fresh-cooked meals,' she declares, pushing the frozen boxes of palak paneer and rajma to the very back of the freezer. 'Your friends, who all sensibly married on time, I bet they don't eat such unhealthy frozen food.' She cooks every day because she abhors day-old food. In India she leaves out all solid leftovers for cows, dogs, and birds; here she leaves them for the birds in his balcony. There aren't enough birds around, so the remains frequently end up in the trash.

'I do make fresh meals now and then,' Ved points out, 'better than many Indian wives I know.' Mother lets out a dismissive shrug. They think that certain tasks do not befit him and his station in life—cooking, dishwashing, laundry; certainly not the cleaning of floors and toilets—jobs more 'natural' for womenfolk or servants. So it pains them to watch him do such work. He cites dignity of labour and argues that he doesn't mind, that he likes being self-sufficient, but his words fall on deaf ears. At least during their visit, they want him to live as an Indian family man ought to: tea in bed, hot meals on the table, no cooking or cleaning chores.

Often, while Ved eats breakfast, Father relays bits of news from the morning's TV. He has heard that California is undergoing a major drought but is mystified to see the city supplying water 24x7. One day, shaking his head dismissively, he said, 'What do these people know about water scarcity? Here it means not watering your lawn every day! Someone should show them what a real drought looks like.'

One day he relayed another story extolling the nutritional merits of fish. Though vegetarian himself, he urged Ved to consume more fish. In support, Mother, also vegetarian, chimed in from the kitchen, 'Yes, fish is very high in phosphorous. That is why the Bengalis are so smart.'

They want him to eat six almonds a day, soaked overnight and peeled. They also try and push Ayurvedic Chyawanprash on him, but he flatly refuses. A large proportion of their conversations revolve around food and dubious theories of nutrition. He can never keep straight their classification of foods into 'hot' and 'cold'. It has nothing to do with temperature, but yet it proclaims some foods more suitable in some seasons rather than others.

On their afternoon walks, they sometimes visit streets with upmarket boutiques. They window-shop, convert prices to rupees, and excitedly relate their findings to him ('a third-class cotton shirt for five thousand rupees!'). With an instinct for thrift honed over a lifetime—one which has long begun to shade into ordinary miserliness—Father still haggles over prices with street vendors back home. Here they return from the shops with mass-produced souvenirs at astonishing clearance prices. On weekends, Ved takes them for grocery shopping and local sightseeing.

Father has also started picking up free local rags from somewhere, with movie and theatre reviews and all manner of classifieds, which he then reads diligently. Every so often, engrossed in their pages, he turns positively wide-eyed. Ved wonders whether he is reading the adult classifieds section: escort girls ready to indulge his every sexual fantasy; lonely housewives seeking a good time in the afternoons; how a leather-bound lady with a whip, sadistic yet caring, wants to turn him into a weak-willed toy for her pleasure.

He studies used car prices, housing market dynamics, free events and concerts. Ved has told them that his rent is half of what it actually is, but they still think it's too much. One evening Father asks, 'Property prices have shot up 12 per cent in the last six months alone. Why don't you buy a house, beta?'

'I don't want a house, papaji,' Ved replies, 'It will tie me down. I don't care about home ownership, nor do I want the mundane worries that will follow. If I have to look after a house, the house will own me instead.'

'Ajeeb baat karte ho, beta!' he says, shaking his head ruefully. 'I don't understand you anymore. Your thinking has become so peculiar and idealistic, so detached. Like a sadhu's. All of your friends have bought houses. They don't spend their valuable time and money on reading and travelling to third-class countries. You need to be worldlier and more practical.'

Ved takes them to a community college for a free classical music concert that Father found in one of those weekly rags. During the piano solo, Father dozes off, slumped in a corner seat near the back. He wakes up when a duo arrives to perform a piece on violin and piano. 'Great jugalbandi!' he observes at its conclusion.

Ved brings home exotic fruits and drinks and takes them to sample a different cuisine each week: Thai, Mexican, Italian, Ethiopian, Moroccan, and others. Eating out was never something they did out of choice, and they approach it now with clinical interest. They complain about the prices in most restaurants and, based on their own dishes, assess the cuisines of entire nations. Long ago, when he was a child, they exposed him to whole new ideas, foods, and experiences. That he can reciprocate today brings him a measure of pride and satisfaction.

Father admires many aspects of the West and of America in particular: its prosperity and hi-tech innovation, law and order, its efficiency, and how resolutely it wages the war on terror. In his State of the Union address, President

Bush said, 'I have no doubts about evil. I know it when I see it. Evil is evil, and we will fight it with all our might. We are a peace and freedom-loving nation but we're not weak. We will chase evildoers to their graves!' The speech brimmed with bluster and jingoism—a President with no doubts about evil? That's the territory of morons and monsters. Yet Father, much to Ved's annoyance, was impressed by the oratory. More often than not, Father uncritically buys the big media viewpoint on current affairs. Ved challenges his take at times, though Father tends to relapse into his comfort zones, which include an increasingly devout, middle-class Hindu outlook, alongside a garden-variety prejudice against Muslims. It is in the air everywhere, in both India and America, and Father too does not escape it.

His parents also admire the privileges and discounts that senior citizens get in the US. They like the cleanliness, orderly traffic, and the honest transactions of daily life. 'No honesty left in India, too much corruption,' Father laments. 'Otherwise, India too would be rich.'

Animating his analysis is the sort of deference and awe, laced with fear and envy, that a small-towner might initially feel in a shiny metropolis. Ved understands it intuitively; it is an echo from his own early days as a graduate student in America.

§

He listens to his parents' running opinions on American society. He probes their assumptions, corrects errors of fact. Their admiration for America doesn't extend to its liberal social mores, particularly those related to sex, marriage and family. As on their previous visit, they make overly generalizing remarks on the extreme solitariness of Americans, their fickle relationships, their self-centeredness. Ved argues back, pointing out the shades of grey.

Truth is that he just can't relate to their idea of a healthy, fulfilling relationship. They subscribe to a Hindu, caste-bound, patriarchal ideal in relationships, rooted in socially sanctioned roles and rituals. Lack of bad news in a relationship implies that all is good. If the muck doesn't float up to the surface, all is good. They think his cousins in India have fulfilling marriages. He thinks the opposite, that most of them are in marriages of convenience at best, not self-aware enough to be good to either themselves or their spouses.

One day, for example, after a news story on the high rates of divorce in California, Father sagely turned to Ved and observed, 'There are very few divorces in India. But I have noticed that even Indians pick up this disease after coming here.'

'Disease? Must a couple stay together if they don't get along? Indian couples aren't any happier than American couples; they just remain together for practical and social reasons, suffering silently, especially women, because of their financial dependence on men.'

'I'm not so old-fashioned,' Father said. 'There are situations when divorce makes sense, but people here don't try hard enough. Every marriage has some problems. One has to make adjustments, sacrifice. But here, they walk out as soon as things turn difficult, or if they get bored, discounting its impact on children. Marriage has become frivolous in America.'

'Papaji, that's a false stereotype,' Ved protested. 'Most people try hard enough and worry about their children. They don't plan on a divorce at the time of marriage. Sometimes it just doesn't work out because people make mistakes in choosing partners, or they grow out of each other and become different people.'

'Become different people? Why doesn't that happen in India?'

'It does happen but to a lesser extent. In India, the individual has been traditionally subordinate to family and social order, so it is harder to go against the tide, to reinvent oneself. But in America, the idea of the individual is idolized. Here, people pursue their own passions and dreams—frequently of dubious merit, yes—but it can create conflict and a falling out with family and social norms. Indian cultural values have long emphasized the opposite.'

'That's why they are better values!' Father asserted. 'That's why Indian culture has lasted so long.'

'Sure, if longevity is the goal of societies, India scores well. But can mere longevity make a culture better for its members? Think about Vandana aunty, a social pariah for years because her husband divorced her. People still call her a divorcee, saying it like it's a curse or a moral deficiency. The stigma ensured that she never got married again, remember?'

'I think the truth is that people here are too selfish,' Father said derisively, ignoring Ved's point. 'They only think about themselves and what's best for them individually. Indian culture is superior. As I said, divorce may be necessary sometimes. But now this divorce trend, much like fast-food, loud music and clothing fashions from America, is spreading to Indian cities too.'

'I am not sure which culture is superior. Indian culture still has dowry, caste barriers and untouchability. Ninety per cent of people still marry within their caste. It has so much superstition, religious polarization, obsession with skin colour, rank and status—'

'Woh theek hai,' Father conceded. 'Fine, so no culture is perfect, but when it comes to marriage and family, Indian culture is much superior. No wonder American children abandon their parents, pushing them into old-age homes and leaving them to die among strangers. But what else should the parents expect? What you sow is what you reap.'

Mother nodded in agreement. 'I would consider living like that a prison sentence,' she said in a rare tone of disgust. He didn't have the heart to point out that so many in India also abuse their parents in old age, a fate generally spared those who live and die in the company of friends or strangers. He saw little point in continuing the debate. This is an issue close to their hearts, and on which their views are settled.

Fortunately, Father was promptly distracted by the local news. A carjacking and high-speed police chase were being telecast live. Next was the story of a woman who heroically fought her obesity, lost 250 pounds, and now conducts inspirational workshops, exhorting women to think of themselves as warriors and to view their bodies as a battleground. Then a preview of the latest alien attack movie, followed by breaking news of a new terrestrial speed record set in Nevada. All punctuated by ads with shiny cars and skinny women. Watching Father mesmerized by all of this stuff, Ved wondered what exactly was going through his head.

§

His parents obsess over his health, diet, hair loss. Mother has brought a fancy bottle of Ayurvedic hair oil from India and frequently threatens to apply it to his head. She frets over how much older he now looks for his thirty-six years. Surely due to his poor diet! Other men his age are so full of vitality and laughter. What is it that plagues him? Why does he seem so preoccupied with vexing thoughts? What good have they done, she asks, all those books on his shelf? They've only turned him into a joyless, brooding philosopher type. No doubt, Mother declares, he is compelled to read because of his boredom and loneliness. If only he would cast aside his stubbornness and bring home a suitable wife.

Soon after their arrival, Father had asked about his work. Is he doing all he can to keep his boss happy? What about promotions? What is the nature of his work? Ved explained as simply as he could: how the Internet works, what Omnicon makes, where he himself fits in the order of things. His parents think he is a bigshot at work, indeed God's gift to Omnicon. He hasn't told them yet that the job they see as shining proof of his success actually means little to him, that he is nothing more than a reluctant and perfectly dispensable foot soldier in the system.

A week ago, he took them to his office at Omnicon. They put on their best clothes to make a positive impression on his colleagues, who offered polite, customary greetings as they passed by in the corridors. They met his boss Roger who gauged the situation and, charmingly enough, gave Ved a glowing review. They listened attentively and were easily impressed. Mother even donned a proud, beatific expression on her face that said: there, that's my son!

All their lives they have exulted in his achievements: honours and awards as a student, now promotions and raises. In his extended family, he is regarded as a major success story—first his admission into one of the top engineering colleges in India, then a scholarship for 'further study' in America, and now an 'important post' in Omnicon, a hi-tech giant well-known even in India. Father boasts about him to anybody polite enough to listen back home—it is his success story too.

By now Ved is all caught up on news and gossip from his extended family, a veritable soap opera brimming with factions, psychological battles and intrigues. Besides the mundane updates on jobs, marriages, newborns, and health disorders, they also span the unsavoury gamut: cousins cheating each other as business partners; bitter fights over a dead parent's patrimony; ungrateful sons stealing their senile father's pension; a daughter-in-law insulted for birthing a girl child. 'See! This too is the Indian family,' Ved cheekily pointed out once.

He is reminded again of the large presence their clan has in his parents' lives, a presence whose complex web of obligations and expectations they both resent and rely on. How immersed they are in the lives of people so peripheral to him. He is saddened by his inexorable drift away from their world and the huge gulf that now exists between them. The only two people who seem to love him unconditionally have no way of tapping into what preoccupies him most of the day. He must spend more time with them in India, he thinks, lest these gaps grow wider.

Mother fasts once a week. Every so often she even fasts for his sake, that is, for the gods to alter his conjugal fortunes. Two or three times she has initiated a conversation about his plans for marriage. Each time, he has managed to deflect the topic. He knows exactly what they will say: If he acts now, he can still get a suitable wife from India. It is not too late. India is full of independent, educated and career-minded girls these days. He must not only settle down but have children too, else he will be full of regrets in old age.

'But children can also be a source of sorrow in old age,' Ved pointed out recently.

'Why must you always imagine the worst possibility?' Father responded with a dismissive shake of his head—a gesture that Ved now associates with Father's refusal to question his own cherished beliefs.

They talk about the ongoing changes in India. Prices have skyrocketed, as have the salaries in the professional classes. Father was a mechanical engineer in a public-sector steel company. What he earned in his final year before retirement, eight years ago, is what fresh graduates from his college now earn in three months. Good thing they built their house when they did and saved for a secure retirement. At least one scourge of old age is unlikely to visit them, as in worrying about money and relying on one's offspring for material sustenance.

They ask if Ved is saving enough. Despite his assurances, they suspect he is a spendthrift, doling out too much on travel and books, and tipping too much in restaurants. He listens with amused indulgence. At times, he marvels at their simple priorities and the spontaneous joy they find in little things, but he knows that this sort of simplicity, too, is not without an underbelly.

§

These differences pale in comparison to the difficulties he had with them on their previous visit five years ago. Those conflicts and memories still occasionally haunt him. That's when they had met Pooja, an episode he can still only remember with bitterness. It revealed to him a whole new facet of them. Words and gestures from that time still echo in his mind.

He had told them about Pooja just days before their arrival. They were ecstatic on the phone—it was the only time he had talked to them about a woman in his life. They were full of anticipation when they landed, eager to meet their potential daughter-in-law. They asked about her even on their ride from the airport. Ved knew they would dislike several things in her family history—her parents, besides being in an inter-religious marriage, were also far more socially liberal—but Ved was determined to lay it all out on the table.

'So here are the basic facts of Pooja's life,' he told them that first evening. 'She was born in the US to Indian parents: Muslim father, Brahmin mother, who met in a US university. As one might imagine, especially in those days, her mother's family did not accept the marriage for years. Pooja grew up in Houston and has only one sibling, a sister.'

He paused, bracing for the trickier part. 'But like all families, they have their issues too. Pooja's parents divorced after twenty years of marriage, so that caused some disruptions.'

'Oh! Why did they divorce?' Father asked. Mother looked on with wide eyes.

'I don't know the details.'

'Did they start living separately too?'

'Yes, the daughters divided their time between them. Their mother never remarried but the father soon married a white American, a secretary in his office.' Their eyes widened further.

'What does her sister do?' Mother asked. 'Is she married?'

'She lives and works in Houston, but is not married. She was married, but not anymore. Now she is raising a child by herself, with her mother's help.' Ved lied, choosing not to reveal that the child had been born out of wedlock.

Noticing their initial excitement deflate sharply, Ved switched gears and said, 'Despite all that, Pooja became an outstanding student, a topper! She holds more academic degrees than me, all from leading American universities. She is very sensible and sober and regularly volunteers her time to help others. Our interests and outlook in life have so much in common.' But all this, Ved noticed, barely made a dent on their now sullen faces.

The following day, Pooja came home to meet them over tea. She wore her favourite leather coat and tights.

His parents struggled a bit with her accent but nothing controversial came up. He thought it all went fine. So he was surprised to discover their disappointment with her, and their vitriolic remarks after she left. Looking positively glum, Mother began with a sigh of resignation, 'She is very cunning. I can see how she has roped you in.'

'What do you mean roped me in?' he was genuinely puzzled.

'Beta, you are too innocent, a simpleton in these matters,' she said. 'She is clearly not good enough for you…she is only using you. She is too American, not sacrificing like Indian girls. Before investing further, test her out.'

Hiding his irritation, he said, 'I've tested her enough, ma.'

'No, you haven't. I don't think she will stick with you in hard times.'

'I think she will,' he said impatiently. 'I'm happy with her.' He said this even though he wasn't sure about their long-term prospects—for reasons very different from his parents'. Their one year of dating so far had not been without its challenges, even though at thirty-one, it had already been his longest relationship.

'I don't see anything special in her. Not even that good looking…she lacks feminine charm and grace, too dark…'

'Too dark?' His ears burned, he took a deep breath. 'Too dark for what? By feminine charm and grace, you mean a fair-skinned Indian doll, with a painted face and girlish giggle, who knows when to shut up in the company of elders, who meekly minds the household. Right?'

'Beta, I know it doesn't feel good to hear this. No one else cares enough to tell you, we are only doing our duty by warning you.' She glanced at Father, trying to solicit his support, 'It is clear that she does not even come from a good family. Look at her father—how disgraceful, divorcing in old age for the sake of physical pleasure.'

'Just look at her sister,' Father jumped in. 'Also divorced! I am sure these values run in her family; this is their family tradition. She will not think twice about betraying you when the time comes.'

Biting his lips, Ved tried to reason with his parents but they were not going to budge. Too late to change their views. Another force, a whole different worldview, spoke through them. It made them oblivious to his arguments.

'This girl is not reliable,' Father declared in a tone of finality, shaking his head in bitter disappointment. 'With such huge differences, how can you two stay together long-term? We had such hopes from you beta, and this is what you bring before us!' Father had a look of genuine bewilderment, 'This?'

'What good are all her degrees? She earns less than you. Are you sure she is not after your money?' asked Mother.

'She is older than you. I heard that an older wife reduces the husband's lifespan,' asserted Father.

'What? Where do you hear such nonsense?' Ved asked with mounting irritation. 'Shashi Kapoor and Sunil Dutt are doing just fine.'

'To make matters worse, she is half-Muslim,' muttered Father. 'She must surely have some Muslim values.'

That drove him over the edge. He practically screamed,

'What do you mean "Muslim values"? Shame on you and your stupid Hindu values!' More recriminations and harsh words followed, until at last, he stormed out to his room. His anger had left him shaking.

In the days that followed, they kept long faces and exchanged hurtful looks. He came home late and left early in the mornings. He had not anticipated such a lopsided reaction to Pooja. It brought home to him that when it came to marital issues, people reveal their true colours, their bedrock views of the world. It filled him with a confused sense of bitterness and loathing. He would walk away with Pooja, he decided, if he were forced to make a choice.

Realizing he was not going to change his mind about Pooja, his parents began worrying about the fallout in their community back home. He had told them that he and Pooja had no fondness for the institution of marriage and did not plan to marry. If the heart and mind are in the right place, what else matters? They don't need others to sanctify their bond. Besides, he said, marriage is no insurance against separation or unhappiness. Why then suffer the whole charade?

'What will people say at home if you cohabitate without marrying? They will laugh and taunt us. Hai Ram! They will say behind our back, "Did you hear their son has taken in a rakhail, a kept woman! Such a nice boy he used to be." They will say that America has totally corrupted you,' Mother said.

'I don't give a damn what they say,' he said angrily. 'It is my life to live, the way I want.'

'See, how selfish he has become,' Father said, glancing

at Mother. 'This is what America has done to him. But we have to live among them, beta. Is this why we sacrificed so much for you, so you can bring this dishonour upon us, such disgrace?' There was melodrama enough to put Bollywood to shame. It left him utterly drained.

'Fine, don't tell them about her,' he proposed. 'Let her be a secret for now.' And that is what they finally settled on. For their extended family, Pooja would not exist. They met Pooja three more times during that visit, but never warmed up to her. They kept searching for an Indian daughter-in-law in her, much to their disappointment. Though Pooja made some allowances for their expectations—doing more in the kitchen, dressing more conservatively—nothing she did was good enough. A huge chasm separated them, mirroring in many ways the cultural chasm between India and America. India came out looking far worse: petty, archaic, heartless.

A year or so later, he told them about his separation from Pooja but didn't provide many details, certainly nothing about her pregnancy or the child. Like many of his friends, they too wouldn't have approved of him 'leaving' her in that situation. They were mostly relieved by the story they heard. Father's words are still etched in his mind. 'Don't worry, beta. She wasn't right for you anyway. Find another girl. So many beautiful and qualified ones are available.'

§

The whole sordid drama over Pooja had forced him to reexamine the very foundations of his relationship with them. Nothing but random chance had brought them together as a family, he thought. In fact, his parents weren't particularly admirable or inspiring human beings. What were his duties and obligations towards those who, were they not tied to him by accident, would hold no special interest to him? Their very existence began to feel like a burden.

Alongside, he also pondered his parents' personal histories, casting his mind's eye on their childhood and youth, reflecting on their modest start as newlyweds in small-town India. He recalled the soul-numbing quality of Father's work—six days a week for four decades, he left early for the heavy engineering plant with its deafening roar of machines. He came home for lunch and then worked again till sundown. What pressures did they live with back then?

Not until Ved was ten did they move up into the middle-class staff quarters for the more senior professionals at his father's company. Ved remembers a labour dispute in which his father was involved. Scores of people gathered outside their house and began chanting angry slogans. For days afterwards, Ved felt a strange menace in the air.

Mother managed the household and her fickle bunch of domestic helpers. For a stretch running into years, his parents quarrelled over things Ved did not understand. He recalls father screaming at Mother once, 'I will leave you to rot till you die!' Twice he even saw bruises on Mother's face. Occasionally when Ved was around during or after a quarrel, Mother would pull him into her embrace and let out a long, muffled cry, as though trying to choose between fitful hiccups and free-flowing tears. Without warning, Father would turn crabby, fume and swear, then bury himself into the *Hindustan Times*. How did they see the world back then and what caused their discords?

He is glad his parents did not part ways, else he may have been deprived of a secure and stable childhood. Beyond the ordinary existential angst of boyhood, he recalls nothing unpleasant enough to haunt him today. He wonders briefly whether their relationship affects his own dealings with women. His parents did their best in raising him, despite their own difficulties and confusions. It could easily have been far worse.

As he dwelled on their past, he began to see his parents in a new light, as small-town people in a fast-changing world, products of a middle-class order whose values and beliefs they had absorbed willy-nilly, and which were now central to their identity. Their struggles differed from his, their lives closer to the margins than his. No wonder they turned out so much more fearful of the unknown. Thanks to them, his own youth had been far more cushioned than theirs. He also saw that in their own way, they had come a long way too.

It later struck him that despising his parents for their provincial views was hardly heroic. Is this what all his 'learning' has taught him? It was now almost four years since he started making peace with it and began to accept them as they were. He began to engage them once again, this time more as an adult, relating to them not as lamentable departures from some concept of 'ideal parents', but as people with their own worldviews and struggles in life.

§

One evening, Ved plays for them a BBC documentary on evolution. It starts with the timeline of evolution. The earth is five billion years old, dinosaurs lived until 65 million years ago, a time of the early mammals. Hominids evolved only 4–6 million years ago, and modern humans a mere 200,000 years ago. How recent the human species really is!

Watching wildlife provokes in Ved disquieting thoughts once again, as he drifts into a reverie: How blind evolution is, proceeding with utter disregard for our moral imperatives. How all animal organs, abilities, capacities are shaped by the fierce, mysterious will to life, which he shares with all life, indeed all of nature. And how often he forgets this in daily life. All our talk of good and evil, truth and beauty, is a play of words, amid a dance of numbers. To feel this in the bones, and to live with such awareness, is surely to shed a veil of illusion.

His parents watch the entire series mesmerized. Sweeping ocean shots accompany the section on whales. Mother asks, 'Moving in empty space around the sun, how does so much water stick to the surface of the earth, why doesn't it fly away?' She is reluctant to assign all credit to gravity. In her mind, there is another force that makes it all hang together: God.

Ved wonders if evolution is anything more than an academic concept to them, whether they understand its implications for their own origins. Ved knows their sense of history and its scale is weak. Beyond a few generations, the past is hazy, informed by folklore and garish soap operas about gods and kings. After the documentary, Mother asks, 'Didn't demons live a long time ago? If there can be such strange creatures in the deep sea, why not demons? What about Rama and Krishna, exactly how long ago did they exist?'

Though he believes it's never too late to explore the big questions, he searches for an honest response that won't rudely destroy their fond illusions and leave them worse off. It behooves him to tread with care. Rather than merely dismissing their views, he should focus on nudging them towards a more truthful view.

'Scientists believe that demons have never existed,' he says. 'Nor have historical records turned up any evidence for the existence of Rama and Krishna, but both Indian epics, written by poets some two thousand years ago, could well have been inspired by actual events. However, Buddha and Mahavira existed for sure, as did Jesus and Mohammed.'

They mull his response. The topic somehow shifts to reincarnation. They profess their hesitant belief in it, and the 'evidence' they cite is the usual kind—hearsay about some villager who verily 'remembered' his former life and returned to meet his ex-relatives, who apparently corroborated all his memories. Ved listens politely, tinged once again by a measure of sadness at the distance he and his parents have travelled apart.

§

Sasha calls during the week. She sounds excited and wants to talk to him about something. 'Are you free for dinner?' They agree to meet at a Thai restaurant downtown. He calls his parents to say that he will return late—his boss is taking out his team for dinner.

He parks in a multi-storied garage and finds her waiting for him at the restaurant. She reveals her big news: George, after their last two weeks together in Boston, has proposed marriage. The day she landed, he got them both tested for HIV. This is the first time she has taken an offer of marriage seriously. She is confused, unsure what to do. What does he think?

She pulls out a picture of George taken in Costa Rica. A short stout man, pale skinned, with a broad smile. He could well be a high school baseball coach.

'Are you in love with him?'

She shrugs, 'He says he is in love with me.'

'Do you believe him?'

'I don't think he is lying. He is nice enough. I can live with him.'

'Why are you even considering this? Why not wait for someone you respect, someone you can truly fall in love with?'

She sighs, 'I am not sure that will ever happen. I am tired of my job. I can't do this forever. I want to be an artist. George thinks I should take art classes at a college in Boston. If I don't try it now, it will be too late.'

'Will he sponsor you for a Green Card?'

'Yes. In the meantime, I can do my art course and explore my talent.'

'That sounds convenient. Two birds with one stone. Just don't rush into kids.'

'He does not want kids. He has one from his previous marriage.'

'What are you worried about then?

'Well, it is a big step, you know. I want it to work

out, at least for some years. He is a nice man. The only negative I've found is that he is not too open-minded about other cultures and foreigners, like Arab people, also Indian people. We argued about it in Costa Rica.'

'Guess he and I won't have much to talk about.'

'"I have nothing to learn from Arabs and Indians," he said. But he is critical of many Americans too, the religious kind. He says he is smart enough to see through the bullshit of both political parties. Both of them frighten him. He calls himself a libertarian who votes Republican.

'He also wants to sign a prenuptial agreement, which I had never even heard of in Russia. I don't like it but I can understand. His ex-wife got a lot of his money from their divorce.'

They eat for a while in silence and then discuss the pros and cons of the choices facing her. He can see that the odds are heavily stacked in favour of her accepting his offer. He looks up and sees in her a fiancée of someone named George, who is not fond of Indians.

He pays the bill, they step out. 'Well, let me know when you have decided.'

'I think it's mostly decided,' she says softly.

The fog is rolling in now, there is a cool ocean breeze. He looks at her and is suddenly seized by a jealous desire. He wants to fuck her one last time, before she, George's fiancée, leaves to become his wife.

In the elevator to his parking floor, he draws her close and proposes a quickie in his car. She is wearing a skirt, it shouldn't be too hard, he says. 'I'm tired, can we just go?' She resists by pushing against him, then yields reluctantly. His car is in a poorly lit corner of the sixth floor. The mall has closed; few cars remain. Pushing back the passenger side seat, he seats himself and coaxes her on top.

Her lower back is cool and damp. He pulls down her panties and slips on a condom. Stoked by the novelty of place, his lust is needy and urgent. She barely reciprocates and is impatient for him to finish. He knows that at this very instant, she does not want it. Despite a nagging voice in his head, he does not stop.

In less than two minutes he is done. She pulls down her skirt and slips out of the car with a hasty goodbye, without her customary parting kiss, even before he has pulled off the condom.

Stupid mistake, he knows instantly, watching her recede in the distance. What power possessed him? He is stricken with remorse and fear. What hope does he have in the face of these passions that besiege him still?

§

Midway into his parents' stay, Vikram invites them home for dinner. Driving there, Ved grows anxious about it. Vikram has a tall, light-skinned, North Indian wife with just the sort of domesticity that appeals to Mother. They have two children, two big cars, a huge entertainment centre in a large double-story suburban house, with two circular staircases coming down as in Bollywood movies, and a well-appointed puja ghar. It is bound to push all of Mother's buttons.

The evening goes as Ved feared. He can see that his parents are impressed by the décor, plush furniture, shiny electronics, Indian art and the BMW in the driveway. They are further impressed when they notice Vikram's name on the cover of a handbook on routing algorithms.

Vikram's wife is decked out in a sari and has cooked an elaborate meal. Their kids, egged on by doting parents, perform before the guests. One plays the guitar, the other piano. Vikram talks about local Indian events: concerts at the India Cultural Center, professional networking events, Holi at the Hindu temple. He complains that Ved attends none of them.

'Why aren't you normal like your friends?' Mother demands on the way home. 'Just look at you,' she says, 'still living like a student in a small apartment, with cheap furniture, old car. As it is, you have few friends left. You don't realize it now but without a family, you will be terribly lonely in old age. Then you will regret having squandered your life on travel and books.'

At home, before going to bed, Mother remarks in a melancholy tone that perhaps they should never have encouraged his going to America. Perhaps then he would not have become so strange. He would have found a good enough job in India, married a local girl, and sired two children by now. Just like his cousins and friends.

'Ma, it has nothing to do with America,' he jokes. 'Vikram turned out normal, didn't he? I'm following another Indian—the Buddha. Remember he too renounced family life and chose to live in solitude and simplicity?'

'He is not a good role model in this respect,' she declares. 'That's what he chose to do. Of all people, why do you imitate him?'

'Well, the real reason is that for all the trouble I have been to you, I am determined not to let my offspring do the same to me.' He said it as a light remark, but Mother turns melodramatic and starts weeping. He backpedals, insists it was a joke, and tries to make her smile. Even now, every time she breaks down into tears, her sorrow unsettles him deeply.

§

His parents' bickering and pestering each other, he believes, lends a structure to their lives. He wonders if they can now live without it. Nowadays, whenever they argue about something in his presence, they both try to recruit his support. He finds this nothing short of endearing. How will the one who outlasts the other cope with being alone?

Their health disorders always concern Ved. Father has high blood pressure and struggles with heartburn and early stage arthritis. Mother has high blood sugar, frequent backaches, and mild asthma. His dadaji had Parkinson's and his naniji suffered from senile dementia. One masi had colon cancer. All this, then, is in the domain of what might inflict him too.

He worries about his parents' final years. How will his life change when only one of them is left, say, his mother? He feels guilty for not being around them much to care for them. When his father gloats about his achievements back home, some people must whisper behind his back: a deserter son, too selfish, alienated from Indian values.

Come what may, he tells himself, he will shepherd them through their second childhood. It will not be easy, but he wants to be there, as they were when he needed them most. Nothing he is involved with will be more important than helping them through the end. He wants to do it, no less for himself and his idea of what one generation owes another.

Twelve

FATHER KNOCKS FRANTICALLY ON HIS door one morning, 'Wake up, beta! Your CEO has been fired, along with three other executives.'

Ved springs out of bed and finds the story on another channel. It turns out that last week, Omnicon's chairman got wind of grave accounting 'irregularities' at the company. An emergency weekend audit confirmed it, revealing the extent to be billions of dollars. Heads have rolled as a result. There will likely be a restatement of earnings for the past 6–8 quarters.

The stock market has taken the news badly. It has come at the heels of other corporate accounting fraud cases. Trading in Omnicon shares was halted when the price tumbled by a third in the opening minutes. 'What will happen?' Mother asks worriedly. 'Your stock options are now good for nothing. You are just like your father! He too doesn't know how to sell at the right time.'

Ved combats his parents' anxiety with affected mirth, 'Arre, no need to worry! These things happen now and then. Omnicon has good products. The new management will soon fix all problems. The shares will recover in a few months, just wait and see.' Silently he curses Greg and his coterie of crooks.

There is only one topic of discussion at work. Rumour mills remain strong; people huddle in small groups in hallways and the cafeteria. It seems Omnicon's accounts had been doctored for up to two years. Its actual performance was far worse. The boys slid past fiscal creativity into corporate crime. The management had hyped Omnicon's growth prospects so much that many employees had invested huge portions of their 401(k) retirement savings in company stock.

At midday, he calls his parents and tells them once again to not worry, that his colleagues, though a little shaken, are taking things in their stride. Since no one is working, he leaves the office early. At home, his parents are hungry for details. 'What does this mean for your job? What will they do to the CEO?'

In the evening business news, an industry analyst talks about Omnicon. He minces no words. It is a major financial scandal. Omnicon has joined the growing ranks of rogue US corporations. Just last month, recalls Ved, this same analyst had upgraded Omnicon's stock. Now he is predicting a long slump, or worse—class-action lawsuits, possibly driving the company to seek bankruptcy protection. The story further raises his parents' anxiety.

The analyst continues, 'Looking at their history and acquisition trail, we see a classic wheeler-dealer in the CEO. A VP who quit Omnicon last year had questioned his business ethics and called him "a dodgy man."' More sleazy details emerge on the fallen hero: his extravagant lifestyle, homes, yacht, ex-supermodel wife. The same gang of analysts had hailed Greg as a visionary two years ago. Now they're busy dishing up dirt on him.

'I always assumed Omnicon was a good company,' Mother says in a sad voice.

'I thought we Indians had a monopoly on corruption,' Father jokes, hiding his anxiety.

§

Early in the week, he rings Sasha several times but she does not pick up. When he rings her apartment, her Ukrainian roommate says that Sasha is not around, nor does she know her whereabouts. His fears are confirmed: Sasha is avoiding him.

As the week goes by, he finds that his parents cannot stop fretting over the fate of Omnicon and his job. To create a diversion, he rents two recent Bollywood blockbusters. He had seen their posters at the local Indian store and his parents had heard good things about them.

To his chagrin, the first film is about a wayward son studying in America, while his parents pine for him in India. Seduced by America's glitter, he forgets his wholesome Indian values and falls in thrall to crooked white women. A horde of blonde bimbos tries to seduce the hero, but after the inevitable treachery of the blondes, the desi lad regains his senses, returns home, and promptly falls for the community belle—a paragon of modesty, virtue, and sweetness. Squirming in his seat Ved wonders whether, from his parents' point of view, a story and its implicit sermons can get any more relevant.

At least there aren't any sexual or wet-sari scenes; he still feels awkward watching anything even mildly erotic with his parents. A handsome bad guy soon appears with designs on the girl, who, spurning our US-returned hero, falls for the bad guy's dangerous charm. But the hero, surprisingly adept in martial arts, puts his life on the line to save the girl when the bad guy's true colours are revealed to her. Though alone and unarmed, he beats up the villain and his dozen cronies armed with hockey sticks, bicycle chains and broken glass bottles. Finally, a tearful union with the weepy, repentant girl paves the way to a happy ending.

The usual Bollywood melodrama, Ved shakes his head, with hokey moralizing through characters that are either good or bad, virtuous or corrupt. Little is morally ambiguous. The hero makes mistakes, which he then rectifies, but shows no real inner conflicts. It still has all the absurd coincidences, clichéd ideas about love and family, *haute couture* changed in mid-song. Nevertheless, the movie manages to engage his parents.

Film production, he notes, has become slicker, sets more elaborate, special effects more hi-tech than he recalls from films in his childhood. Beauty ideals have moved closer to those of Hollywood: skinny women, six-pack men. The young are hipper, and their manner, speech and attire are open tributes to American pop culture. Music too has turned loud and raucous, a far cry from the melodies of his youth.

They watch another movie the following day, about an urban middle-class couple on the verge of retirement. They seem to have no savings because they spent it all on their children's upbringing, counting on a payback in old age. But when they enter retirement, the children are ungrateful, selfish, and treat them badly. Even strangers are kinder to them, one of whom gets the old man to write the story of his life. Though the old man has written little besides office memos as an adult, he churns out a Booker-Prize-winner, instantly making him rich and famous. When the children come and repent at their parents' feet, their father does not forgive them. Only their mother's heart melts.

When Ved points out that the old man's novel is written in Hindi and hence ineligible for the Booker Prize, Mother, annoyed by his nitpicking, says, 'Just assume that he has won some major prize.' The movie has too many contrived tear-jerker moments. While Mother sniffles audibly, Father does it discreetly. Occasionally, the pathos even draws Ved in and he has to struggle to avoid turning misty-eyed. Reflecting on it later, he is quietly amused.

§

One evening, having run out of milk, Ved walks with his parents to Baldev's corner store. Baldev is behind the counter as usual. He greets Ved's parents with a namaste and exchanges a few polite words. When they do not see low-fat milk in the refrigerators, Ved returns to ask Baldev. A few more customers have just entered the door.

'Koi gal nahin,' Baldev replies cheerfully. 'There is more in the other fridge in the back room. I'll get it for you in a moment.' Baldev gets busy servicing other customers. Ved asks his parents to select an ice-cream to take home and, rather than bugging Baldev again, himself goes to the back room and finds the fridge.

Amid stale odours and stacks of cartons, Ved suddenly spots Rashmi sitting on a chair. Anita is on the floor, playing with a toy. Ved can see that Rashmi has a black eye. He walks up to her.

'Hello, how are you? I haven't seen you in a while.'

Rashmi looks at him with a mixture of fear and anguish, says nothing. He notices that she might be pregnant again. Why the hell did Baldev do this to her and bring her to the store? Wouldn't people notice her black eye and ask about it? Is that why he has consigned her to the back room?

'Yeh kaise hua?' Ved asks, pointing to her eye. 'Who did this to you?'

She averts her eyes. He waits for her to speak but she says nothing. 'Did he do this?' he finally asks, pointing his finger towards the storefront.

All at once, she begins to sob. Seeing her mother, Anita too starts sobbing. His suspicion is confirmed. Now he too is involved; he can't just abandon her. But how can he help her? He instinctively pulls out his business card and scribbles his home phone number on the back. 'Listen, call me if you want help of any kind, okay? I know an organization called Saheli, run by Indian women, that can help you.' She takes his business card.

'He gets very angry at me sometimes,' she says weakly. 'Especially when he drinks.'

'Think about what I said, okay? These days you don't have to put up with this. It is okay to ask for help. By the way, my ancestors were from Punjab. I still have some relatives in Punjab,' he says, trying to make her feel at ease. 'But I don't speak Punjabi. My grandfather left Punjab long ago and I grew up in Agra.'

As he is about to exit the back room he looks at her, smiles, and waves his hand. Donning a half-smile, she too raises her hand and waves back.

Walking home, Ved tells his parents about the encounter.

'That's how it is in the lower classes,' Father observes, 'beating their women and such.'

'Not so,' Ved asserts. 'Lots of doctors and engineers are also guilty of domestic abuse.' Has his father forgotten that he too, long ago subjected his own wife to domestic abuse? He and his parents have never talked about it, nor does Ved have the stomach to bring it up now. Ved then reveals that he gave his business card to Baldev's wife.

'Why?' Father asks with genuine surprise.

'Why not? She looked like she might need some help. If she does, she can call me.'

'But that's inviting trouble. He seems like a tough fellow, why get involved with him? It is a private matter. It'll sort itself out.'

'Papaji, how long would you stay silent if you saw domestic violence in your neighbour's house? What if you had a daughter who was the victim and no one else intervened to help?'

'I don't want to argue,' Father mutters irritably and averts his eyes. 'Do as you please.' They walk back in silence. Ved is painfully aware that when it comes to helping others, his own record is not much better than his father's. Indeed, when was the last time he truly went out of his way to help someone unrelated to him?

'You did the right thing, beta,' Mother says on the steps leading up to his apartment. 'Just be careful. We live so far away. Now you have given us another reason to worry about you.'

§

At work, his premonitions of worse times are soon confirmed. The acting-CEO says that Omnicon needs to 'mold itself' for the shifting realities of business, which means another layoff is coming. Language, Ved reflects, is so malleable and corruptible. Euphemisms have turned the Iraq war into an 'engagement'; aerial bombardment has become 'air support'; prisoners are 'detainees.' Mr Orwell must be rotating non-stop in his grave these days.

Industry analysts, too, predict sizeable cuts for Omnicon, especially in marketing and sales. Employee morale has hit rock bottom. Many are polishing their résumés and digging up old contacts. With survival uppermost in their minds, most people have turned secretive about their plans.

Friday morning at work, Ved discovers a message from Sasha on his office voicemail. She is leaving for Boston tomorrow, said a brisk goodbye and wished him luck in his personal life. He calls her back but does not find her. He leaves a voicemail: 'Congratulations on your decision! Please call me before you leave.'

A while later, Roger calls him into his office. Roger suspects that Ved's role will be eliminated. 'I encourage you to explore other jobs within Omnicon. Layoffs could hit as early as a couple of weeks.' Roger promises to help to the best of his abilities but Ved knows that there is little Roger can do, what with his own survival battles. Going forward, each is on his own.

Ved is rattled by this news and goes out for a long lunch over a glass of wine. The best short-term strategy, he decides, would be to try and find a foothold inside Omnicon, and to stay employed for a while, at least until his parents leave in two weeks—they won't be able to handle his layoff, and their worries will only cause him more heartache. For the remainder of the afternoon, he sifts through the internal job postings but finds nothing attractive enough.

§

After the dismal week at work, Ved is already looking forward to the long weekend ahead, and to the trip he has planned with his parents to Lake Tahoe and Reno. On his drive home, Sasha calls.

'I got your message.' Her voice is flat and impassive.

'Listen,' he clears his throat and says, 'I'm sorry about our last time, the way we ended the evening. I don't know what came over me. I'm really sorry.' There is an audible sigh from Sasha, followed by a brief, loaded silence. 'Can I take you out for dinner tonight?' He will behave this time, he wants to add but does not.

'Unfortunately, I can't go. I still have a lot of packing to do.'

'No time for even a quick meal? How about that burrito joint near your place?'

'No, I can't,' she says, 'I have left too much for the last minute.' There is silence for a few seconds. This is clearly not one of their normal conversations.

'So,' he tries to sound normal, 'you are off tomorrow. That must be exciting. When is your next visit to San Francisco?'

'I don't know. I have nothing to come back to.'

'When do you think you'll get married?'

'If all goes well, maybe in two–three months,' she

sounds eager to wrap up the call. 'Listen, I must go now. Take care of yourself.'

'We must keep in touch, at least via email. Best wishes for your new life.'

Poor woman, he thinks: to be forced by life into one hard choice after another, so often wrapped up with the baser instincts of men. Men like him, yes. He gives her a warm mental hug. It strikes him that he may never again see or talk to her. Indeed, at this point, why would she want to see him ever again? The thought leaves him feeling dejected and drained.

§

Friday evening, the media is again abuzz with stories on Greg Dyer. A video has surfaced with scenes from his wife's thirtieth birthday party in Sardinia the previous year. It reveals a fleet of hired yachts, chariot-themed furniture in a pool-side garden of a palatial villa, scantily-clad female 'gladiators' serving hors d'oeuvres, an ice sculpture of Michelangelo's David urinating a vodka punch. Total cost $1 million, half of which was billed to Omnicon as a business expense.

Ved's parents watch a fresh round of exposés and commentary on TV. In another report, a US Congressman has accused Omnicon of aiding the Chinese government's crackdown on dissidents. Omnicon's stock has fallen to $12, down from last week's $26 and its pre-9/11 high of $96. A class action lawsuit has been filed. The odds of bankruptcy have increased. Competitors are rumoured to be putting on their vulture hats, ready to pick on Omnicon's choicest parts. Ved notices another odd spectacle. The surviving members of the executive team are falling over each other to say, 'I accept responsibility.' Just to be able to say those words has become a mark of status, honour and integrity. But none of them, Ved acidly observes, are willing to resign or be otherwise penalized in any way.

Before dinner, his parents finish packing for their weekend trip. They are both eager and anxious about their biggest road trip of this visit. They retire early with the goal of leaving early in the morning.

Thirteen

HIS PARENTS LOVE THE GORGEOUS mountain scenery on the way up to Lake Tahoe. The day is sunny, their spirits are high, and the drive is smooth. Ved takes them on a sunset cruise on the lake. Filled with awe and delight, they stay out on deck the whole time, marvelling at the alpine scenery and the lake's deep blue water, said to be pure enough to drink.

They stay in a B&B with a view of the Sierra Nevada range. Sunday morning, while Ved sleeps, his parents go for a walk. They return with their faces glowing pink from the cold and enjoy hot tea in the room with digestive biscuits. After a breakfast of pancakes and fruits, he takes them on a cable car ride to a high vista point overlooking the lake.

In the afternoon, they cross into Nevada and drive along the lake, stopping at occasional picnic spots and campgrounds, where they pull out the snacks they've brought from home. Finding decent vegetarian food is a small challenge. Their options mostly end up being pizzas, cheese sandwiches, fries and bland salads.

Late afternoon they set off for Reno. They arrive well before sundown and stay in a tall, glittering casino hotel. Casinos depress Ved, with their relentless clink of coins, blinking lights, and glassy-eyed gamblers sitting before slot machines emitting silly, repetitive sounds. He chose this place because of his parents, to show them a piece of Americana that everyone has heard of, this loud, decadent America that simultaneously repels and seduces the world.

After a little rest, they go out to see the evening glitter. They stop to see a live band in a side street, many in the audience drinking beer and swaying to the music. 'People enjoy so fully in this country,' Father notes with approval. The streets throng with people who wander in and out of neon-draped casinos. One casino has a circus act with a sickly Indian elephant they commiserate with. Another casino has an acrobatic show with gasping crowds, much like the crowds around trapeze artists in rural India.

After a pizza and pasta dinner, they saunter back to their hotel, walking by a seedy area, past drunks, pawn shops and prostitutes. He doubts that his parents can identify even the most obvious of hookers, but they do steal glances at the women and walk a bit faster around them.

In their hotel, his parents settle down before two nickel slot machines. With childlike joy, Mother reports her wins to Ved. It brings her no small delight to end the evening with a small profit, and more importantly, well ahead of Father.

§

Late afternoon on Monday, they head back home to San Francisco. His parents are visibly tired from the weekend outing. Barely ten minutes into the drive, Father dozes off in the back seat, Mother sits in the front. He plays a North African music compilation on his car stereo that Liz had gifted to him. He wonders how she is dealing with their breakup.

Shortly before twilight, halfway into the drive, he stops at a gas station to stretch his legs and get a soda. He can see the distant lights of a small town. The parking lot is empty, save for a pickup truck. His parents express no desire to get out of the car. He steps out and hears the roar of the Interstate.

Two young men in tank tops stand beside the pickup, talking and drinking beer, music pounding from the truck. Both look buff and have tattooed arms. They stare at him as he passes. It is not a friendly gaze.

'Hey mister, you Arab?' one man asks, pronouncing it 'ay-rab'. The other one guffaws.

Ved can feel his earlobes heating up but he keeps walking, ignoring them. Entering the store, he takes a few deep breaths. He stops by the refrigerator to pick up a Diet Coke. There is no one at the checkout counter so he rings the bell. Seconds later, a middle-aged man comes in from the back door, accepts his payment, and disappears again. Ved steps out towards his car, keeping a discreet eye on the two men.

He notices one of them moving across his path. A moment later, when they are closer, the man repeats, 'Are you Arab, mister?' His voice, louder this time, betrays a slur. His chin is smooth and shiny; he is much bigger than Ved and has a vaguely menacing look. Ved continues to ignore him and is about to pass him.

'Hey, talk to me,' the man says, sauntering directly in front of Ved, blocking his path.

'About what?'

'You heard me, didn't ya? Are you Arab?'

'What if I am?'

'Then go home, you goddamned Arab,' he hisses. 'Get your stinking ass out of here.'

The second man tries to pull him back. 'Eddie, cut it out, man. Let's go.'

Ignore him, slink away quietly, says a voice in Ved's head. Swallow your pride, step off the path, and use a different way to get to your car. In a few days, you'll probably forget this ever happened. But a strange force stops him. It keeps him standing there facing the man, with a kind of physical courage he didn't think was in him. Not long ago he might even have called it foolish. Now he speaks in a clear, steady voice, 'I live and work here legally. I'm not going anywhere.'

The second man tries to restrain the first. Raising his voice, the second man turns to Ved and says, 'Get away, move!'

Ved moves back two steps but does not go away. He stands facing them in the middle of the path.

Eddie suddenly breaks free and lunges at Ved. The second man tries to contain him again, 'Eddie! Stop!'

But it is too late. A powerful punch lands on Ved's mouth. He averts his face in pain and steps back instinctively. There's blood on his lips, and now on his fingers too. The Coke can has slipped out of his hand, but Ved is not far enough to avoid the next blow. Eddie's hard thump on his back sends him crashing face down to the ground. He hits the curbstone and feels something break; a stabbing pain shoots out from his mouth, just as Eddie lands a hard kick in his stomach. Ved collapses and loses consciousness.

He revives after what seems like minutes, with his torso stretched across his mother's lap. She is frantically trying to revive him by gently slapping his cheeks. Blood is streaming down his face and onto her sari. Father is inside the store, while the manager calls 911. Ved turns over and coughs out a mouthful of blood.

To his horror, he discovers with his tongue that his three front teeth are missing. Instinctively and without a sound, he rolls out of his mother's lap and spits out more blood. His head feels heavy, his nose, jaw and upper lip hurt badly. In the dim light of the parking lot, left hand covering his mouth, he gropes with his right hand for his missing teeth. Despite his grim state, he is relieved to find all three of them in a small pool of blood. He pockets them silently as if they were dimes he had dropped.

Is this just a terrible dream from which he will shortly be rescued?

He looks around—twilight, the empty parking lot with gasoline dispensers and trash bins, the hum of the highway. Mother, her arm supporting his back, appears to be in shock. She is wailing loudly. He tries to calm her down. As he spits out more blood into her handkerchief, the whole incident flashes in his mind. There is no trace of the pickup truck. Only a few empty beer cans lie where the truck had been. The gas station attendant has appeared with a wad of cotton wool which Ved presses against his face.

Two police cars and an ambulance soon arrive with blaring sirens. Three paramedics assess his state and get to work. Ved howls in pain as they hold him down and apply medicated gauze pads on his gums and lips to reduce the bleeding. The cops cordon off a section of the parking lot, gather physical clues, take photos, and talk to the store manager. Two other cars have pulled in from the highway and their passengers are watching the spectacle.

The paramedics drive him to a hospital about twenty minutes away. His parents follow behind in a police car with their bags, leaving their car in the gas station's parking lot.

In the emergency room, a nurse named Kathy x-rays his upper jaw and nose. She asks about the incident and is duly agitated by his account, 'What a nightmare!' she says, shaking her head in disgust, 'Sometimes I wonder where this country is heading.'

A doctor soon arrives, inspects his nose and mouth, and injects a painkiller into his gums. The doctor reports a small crack in his nasal bone and damage to nasal cartilage, but no evidence of a blood clot on the nasal septum. At least the jaw bone doesn't seem to be fractured, says the doctor, but Ved must see an ENT specialist and a dental surgeon by the next day for the right course of treatment and reconstructive surgery.

Ved again attempts to feel the missing teeth with his tongue—hoping against hope that they would magically be there—only to recoil from the hideous wound. He falls back on the bed, exhausted. After local anaesthesia, the doctor puts six stitches on his upper lip and fresh layers of gauze. His wounds seem under control now, but his nose, jaw and head still hurt badly.

From the window in his room, he notices his parents

waiting outside. Father is sitting at the edge of his seat. They look terrified and lost. Suddenly his heart goes out to them. His ordeal has been no less traumatic for them. He imagines Mother watching the assault from the car and then rushing to his aid screaming in a mix of Hindi and English—more of Hindi; her English always fails her in times of distress. He imagines her dropping down onto the curb beside him, laboriously turning his torso around and onto her lap, perhaps with Father's help. How frightening that must have been for them. All at once he has to fight to retain his tears.

'Can I invite them in?' he asks Kathy, straining to speak through the gauze.

'Your parents? Oh gosh, were they with you when this happened?' she asks. 'I'll bring them over.'

Their pained expressions intensify as soon as they set their eyes on him. They rush to his bedside and ask about his state. Mother's forehead is bare; she has managed to lose her ever-present red bindi.

'Don't worry ma'am, your son will be fine,' Kathy says, taking Mother's hand. She listens to his parents' version of events in their hesitant English. 'I am really sorry you had to go through this on your vacation,' she says in a deeply sympathetic voice. 'This is not a common crime in our country. Not yet anyway. I hope they find those men and punish them.'

Kathy then steps out and returns with two cups of tea and a candy bar. His parents are visibly soothed by her kindness. She gives Ved strong painkillers and anti-inflammatory medicine, and advises a good night's rest. If his headache persists in the morning, especially if accompanied by a vomiting sensation or dizziness, he should see his doctor without delay.

Outside the emergency room, he provides a detailed statement to a cop, who reveals that the store's closed-circuit camera was on and will be examined in detail. Ved may be asked to identify the two men if necessary. They agree to be driven by the cop to a nearby motel. The receptionist helps Ved arrange an early morning taxi to San Francisco and to have his car transported back the following day.

§

They reach San Francisco by eleven the next morning. He feels dizzy the entire way and his headache remains acute. He calls Roger but his phone is switched off. Ved leaves a voicemail saying that he has had an accident, 'Don't worry, it's not serious, but it has rendered me immobile this week. Call if you need something,' he pauses, then adds with a forced chuckle, 'or if I no longer have a job.'

Leaving Mother home, Ved and Father take a taxi to the dental surgeon's office. After examining him, the surgeon rises with a sigh, shaking his head, 'That's quite bad. We're looking at a bridge and an implant. Prepare for multiple visits over the next two months.' Ved shows him the three broken teeth he had salvaged.

'Ah, too bad!' the surgeon says. 'They might have been useful had you immediately soaked them in milk to prevent the tissue from drying out.'

'Perhaps I should save these as Central Valley souvenirs,' Ved jokes. They set up their first appointment in two weeks—his injured gums need to heal before any surgical work.

Ved's primary doctor runs various neurological and cognitive tests followed by a CT scan. The results suggest a mild to moderate concussion. For starters, he prescribes complete physical and mental rest for a week. Full recovery could take weeks to months. He asks Ved to see an ENT specialist as soon as his nose swelling reduces.

Despite his protests, his parents get their departure date extended by two weeks. They say they're in no hurry to get back and would rather care for him here. But the wind has clearly gone out of their sails; they seem shaken to the core. They sit around glumly, fret over his condition, rehash the incident, and surf channels on TV. They're no longer eager, perhaps even afraid, to go out and explore the neighbourhood on their walks. Instead, Father has taken to pacing the living room. He seems years older at once.

They start drawing much larger conclusions than warranted. 'This country is no longer safe for Indians,' says Father. He had always heard but wilfully ignored the idea that there was prejudice against brown-skinned people in America. Now that has been made horrifyingly real. Their idea of America has turned on its heel forever.

Of course, the Omnicon saga didn't help either. All told, their faith in his haloed milieu in America now lies shattered. Unlikely that Father would henceforth sing of his son's triumphs to friends and relatives back home. Their mood darkens further when one day they hear about a hate crime on TV in which a turbaned Sikh was fatally shot in Texas.

'I think you should wind up here and return to India,' Father suggests, 'There are lots of well-paying jobs there now.' Besides, he points out, Ved has no big investment in the US to hold him back, by which he means investment in property or family life.

'I do think about returning to India someday,' Ved says honestly, 'but I'll do so on my own terms, at the right time.' He argues that such intolerance is everywhere, thriving on fear and ignorance. Like common passions, racial and religious hatred too can arise anytime, anywhere. When that happens, those outside the mainstream get mauled. Even in India, so many suffer that fate daily, especially among the poor, Dalits, Adivasis, Muslims and women. He points out that prejudice against dark skin is strong in India too. What remains unsaid in their discussion is that Ved is the least likely to suffer that fate in India because he'll be part of the dominant cultural group—light-skinned Hindu men of the upper caste and class.

Balaji and Vikram stop by with their wives. They're aghast at his missing teeth, bandaged lip, and bruised nose, and offer help and sympathy. Balaji's wife has brought a boxful of homemade coconut burfis. Sunil is visiting India but sends a concerned email.

Ved is touched by their support and is grateful for their visit. They share other stories of hate crimes and racial prejudices, from schools and workplaces of people they know. Noticing their own mounting anxieties and feelings of vulnerability in their adopted homeland, he feels a reciprocal empathy for them. 'Don't worry, most likely this is a passing phase,' he says, as others nod hopefully. His interaction with the wives too is perhaps the most normal and unselfconscious that he has ever had with them.

Drawing him out alone on the balcony, Balaji shares some news about Pooja. She has just married a white co-worker in Houston and has moved out to live with him in another part of the city. He has heard this from a mutual friend, who was at Pooja's wedding.

'Oh, great. I hope she is able to find the happy family life that she couldn't with me,' Balaji seems not to notice the mix of relief and wistfulness on Ved's face.

Over tea, shortly before leaving, Balaji casually asks, 'Why did they do this to you? You are not even Arab!'

Is it okay to do this to Arabs? Ved wants to ask but does not. Doing so now might end up spoiling an otherwise cordial evening. Besides, it's probably worth giving Balaji the benefit of the doubt on this one.

§

A law enforcement officer calls later in the week. They've identified his assailant through the store's closed-circuit footage. He was seen in the nearby town earlier and they should have him nabbed shortly. He goes by the name of Edward Morris, Arizona-born, twenty-six years old. He is already on their radar for two misdemeanours—assault and battery of a co-worker, and driving under intoxication. They found an unloaded gun legally registered to Eddie plus ten rounds of ammunition in the glove compartment of the vehicle he had been driving.

'Would you like to press for a hate crime prosecution, rather than simple assault?'

'Yes, please.'

'Right sir, that's what I thought. It's the appropriate thing here, but I still need to ask as per our procedures.

Now that I have your information, we'll be referring this case to the local district attorney's office. You should know that even though you are the victim, the criminal case will be prosecuted as People of the State of California versus Edward Morris. You'll, of course, have the option to sue for civil damages later.'

He outlines the steps, from preliminary hearings, to witness testimonies, to filing charges in the superior court, the jury trial and the verdict, and finally a fitting punishment, if he is found guilty, pronounced by the judge.

'How long does it typically take to get a conviction?' Ved asks.

'Weeks to years, depending on the case. If I may say so, you have a pretty solid case, sir. They might even prosecute this as a felony because the battery here occurred with a hate crime. But you should know that only about 10 per cent of all alleged hate crimes lead to convictions. In fact, most hate crimes don't even warrant formal prosecution.' He calls back a few hours later. 'You'll be happy to know, sir, that we have arrested both Edward Morris and his accomplice.'

'Great. His accomplice didn't hit me though; he even tried to stop his friend.'

'Yes, I am aware of your testimony. I'm sure he'll be treated differently.'

'How did Edward Morris react when arrested?'

'He denied it at first. We often see that,' says the officer.

'Do you have a sense of who this guy is? His background, I mean. What's his story?'

'We don't know yet. For now, we'll get him a lawyer and release him on bail.'

For the umpteenth time, Ved recalls Eddie's taunting voice, his menacing look, his furious lunge. Part of it still feels unreal. What is the source of his rage and xenophobia? Did he think he could get away with it? What an idiot!

§

By the weekend, with his recovery on track and the arrest of the two men, Ved's parents finally start to relax a little. Ved accompanies them on short walks and once to the public library. With their impending departure, they also walk down memory lane more often. Mother reminisces about his shyness at school, his fondness for *Sholay* and other Amitabh Bachchan films, his obsession with Phantom and Mandrake comics, how his misshapen head at birth worried them that he would turn out defective. His colic as an infant made it so hard to even feed him. Holding him in her arms for hours, she had to pace up and down the veranda late into the night, just to pacify and put him to sleep, and he wouldn't sleep without holding his favourite toy duck that made a squeaky sound.

He is struck by her cheerfulness in recounting this. There is no trace of a burden or a complaint. An image of her as a young mother from the faded prints of crusty old family albums flashes in his mind. He imagines the time of his birth, what a moment of joy and pride it must have been for her, a vindication of her procreative powers through the birth of a male child.

All his life, he now thinks, he has discounted their role in making him the man he is today. Yes, they fucked him up too, but they also did many things right for which he ought to be more grateful. They whetted his appetite for learning, gave him security and love, taught him to stand up for himself. Even his turn to atheism in his early teens was enabled by their liberal religiosity. Mother's sympathies and instinctive kindnesses to the old, the infirm and street animals resonate in him still. He recalls her indignation at many social injustices. His parents had worked their tails off so that he could go farther than them. They were his whole world once. How else can he reciprocate if not with an equivalent love, steady beyond the conceits of reason? How can he reliably summon and sustain such love?

Fourteen

'WHAT HAPPENED? DID YOU FALL off your bike or something?' people ask him at work. Within a day, his account of the assault has become crisp and efficient, and it evokes incredulous remarks, shock and sympathy. One woman even recoils in horror from his stitched-up lip and missing teeth. Others stare during meetings and in the cafeteria. He feels self-conscious drawing attention for a wound. A few ask about his assailant and express relief at his capture. He thanks them for their concern, but really wants to be left alone.

The morale at the office is as low as ever. People have grown more secretive as they slip in and out of empty conference rooms to make personal calls. No more 'structural adjustments' have occurred, but the handful of internal jobs are vanishing fast. He did lose precious time last week. He scours the listings again and sees one opening in the Services Department that seems like a moderate fit with his skills and experience.

He emails his résumé to the hiring manager, copying Roger. He is elated when a woman from HR calls him the next day to schedule an interview a day later. 'This is the first round,' she explains. 'If you get past the hiring manager, you'll be asked to interview with others.'

§

Ved goes for the interview with a clear and relaxed state of mind. He begins by explaining his injury to the hiring manager, a stout man named Max. Max commiserates then dives right in, 'Let me tell you some quick facts about me.' He reveals that he is forty-nine, still married to his high-school sweetheart, and has two kids in college. He is into extreme sports like rock-climbing, skydiving, dirt biking, and pretty much anything that moves fast. 'I'm also addicted to hi-tech toys and gizmos,' he adds with a school-boyish grin. 'Technology is my second love.'

Max claims to be 'a straight shooter' and likes others who are too. 'One more thing you should know,' he says, 'is that I am big on responsibility. I mean really big. And if I'm not leading by example, you should come and tell me bluntly: Max, brother, you're full of shit!'

Max describes the job next and examines Ved's résumé more closely. 'You are certainly qualified enough for this position. Maybe too qualified.' he declares. 'But tell me, where do you want to be in your profession 3–5 years from now?'

I don't think that far ahead about work, Ved wants to say but does not. 'I hope I continue to earn the trust and respect of my colleagues. I would like to be satisfied with what I do.'

'Fine, but don't you aspire to roles with more responsibility and leadership?' Max asks.

'Not really. I don't see my career as rungs on a ladder. I am not ambitious in that sense.'

'Don't you aspire to get into management? To lead a group? Or strategy?'

'I don't think my talent extends too well in those areas.'

'Fair enough,' Max nods. 'We all have different talents, can't argue with the will of nature,' he smiles. 'Alright, tell me about some of the key accomplishments and failures of your professional life.'

'I have worked across the entire lifecycle of networking technology, from software development to marketing. I have helped launch four products in my career, three of them very profitable—they are on my résumé. As for failings, the most important I believe is this: I have tried but have not yet tamed things like fear, ego, and desire.'

Max raises an eyebrow, 'Is that a failing? Can you even survive without your ego?'

'True, one needs the ego not only to survive but also to become a better person. But I think there is a kind of ego that actually harms us more than we realize, and which gets in the way of humility, kindness and integrity. That's why I said tame rather than eliminate. The same principle also applies to fear and desire.'

'So how do you separate the harmful ego from the good ego?' Max asks, gamely.

'There is no science to answer that precisely. I suppose it comes from knowing ourselves. The more one understands one's place in the cosmic order, the better one gets at it. At least that's my theory.' Ved smiles but his smile is not reciprocated. Instead, Max has a blank look on his face. Oops, thinks Ved, this is not quite how an interview is supposed to go.

'Okay, tell me about your strengths and weaknesses, something more relevant to this job.'

An old trick question, knows Ved. If he is honest about his weaknesses—admitting, for instance, that he is not really into his profession, that he is burned out and doesn't know what else to do—he would never get hired. The only option left is to take one of his strengths and present it as a weakness, or mention a generic weakness that even Max might have.

'I have plenty of weaknesses, I'll give you three: First, I tend to retain ownership and not delegate effectively. Second, I can be an annoying perfectionist at times. Third, I don't like to be micromanaged, for sure. As for my strengths, I can work effectively in a team. I negotiate firmly and honestly. I am diligent and scrupulous in my work. Like you, I'm also big on responsibility. I believe that if it is worth doing, it is worth doing well.'

§

Next morning Ved meets Roger who informs him that Max did not select him, 'I met him earlier today at Gold's gym.'

'What exactly did he tell you?'

'Do you really want to know?'

'Yeah, I'm curious.'

'Okay, your self-esteem is pretty solid, so I'll tell you. He said, "He's not right for my team. He is bright and all, but I think he is on a quest. This is a new launch. I am looking for a truly hungry individual."'

On a quest? What could Max have meant? wonders Ved. Roger looks more disappointed than him.

'Call Zack in the sales training department,' Roger suddenly says. 'I just heard one of his employees is going on maternity leave. If nothing else, he might have some short-term work for you.' He encourages Ved to look outside Omnicon too. Times are tough, Roger says, even he has started looking outside to extend his options.

He and Roger have so little in common, thinks Ved. They are so far apart in their politics and interests. Yet something compels Roger to look after him even as the boat is sinking. A kind of decency, yes. If their roles were reversed, would he have done the same for Roger? People can surprise you, he muses; they are not merely the sum of their shallowest impulses. An image of Eddie, his attacker, flashes through his mind. Eddie, too, cannot be reduced.

Ved promptly contacts Zack and meets him for lunch on Friday. He seems the laid-back type, a native San Franciscan in his early thirties, tattooed and goateed, with style and swagger to match. The job he has is to train Omnicon salespeople on new releases, to get them to understand product features and benefits in-depth, to handle objections from potential customers, and to run effective demos. The new hire will need to run a classroom averaging three days a week.

Zach likes Ved's background and offers him the job. Ved accepts it even though the pay is 20 per cent less. It stings a little to think of it as a demotion. It's temporary, he reminds himself, a foothold while he plans his next move. His first assignment will be in a week for a product he already knows a lot about.

§

The time for his parents' departure comes. It has been a long trip for them; they seem eager to return to their lives back home. Ved too is itching to reclaim his old routine.

He has not told them about his new position at work. They would fret about it needlessly. On the contrary, he has tried to make things at Omnicon appear much rosier than they are. He is amused to think that in doing so, he is acting exactly like the disgraced executives of Omnicon.

Their time at the airport is as he expected. Mother cries intermittently, father remains sombre. They hug him one last time, Mother clutching him tightly, and then enter the security check area. He waits and watches them from the lounge. Amid the sturdier American frames in the queue, how small and vulnerable they look.

Watching them, he recalls other significant partings of their past: the first time he ever left them for a week-long school trip; the time he went away to college far from home; the time he left for the US. The memories leave him with a melancholy ache. They turn back and wave at him before finally disappearing inside. He walks back to his car with a heavy heart. How he had wanted them to return with pleasant memories from this trip. Who knows when they will visit him next—each year it gets harder for them to make this journey across the world.

At home his apartment feels eerily quiet. Their voices still echo in his head. He half-expects them to emerge from the other room. He knows it will be several days before their sounds and shadows fade from his spaces.

§

His first sales training arrives. He has studied his material diligently. With a temporary dental bridge in place, he is also much less self-conscious about his face.

Eight salesmen attend his three-day class. His job is to

educate them on the latest features of a security product. In the past, he has often taught similar audiences, but as the class proceeds, his enthusiasm wanes. Even as recently as a couple of years ago, he took a lot more interest and tried to understand his audience. Now he feels detached, unable to connect with them. It has fizzled out, his old touch. He feels bored, distant, bothered. He gets annoyed more often, loses patience. As the week progresses, he starts taking breaks more often.

A day after the class, Zack calls Ved into his office. The anonymous feedback forms from his session are on his desk. Without saying a word Zack lets Ved review them. They're not flattering.

One says, 'This important position could use someone more dynamic and personable.'

Another says, 'Instructor knows the material but seemed uninterested in teaching.'

Zack leans back in his chair and says that he will be happy to discuss a development plan for him.

All at once, Ved cannot stand it anymore. He dreads the idea of corporate 'development plans'. Truth is that this job is a mismatch with his temperament and interest. It may be time to cut his losses and leave, for his own mental well-being. It may be time to leave Omnicon.

Without much difficulty, he makes up his mind that evening. He returns to Zack's office the next morning and offers his resignation. Zack is taken aback but accepts it with the faintest of regrets. He informs HR who then calls Ved to schedule an exit interview that same afternoon.

Ved stops by Roger's office to tell him his decision.

'Yep, that training job is not for everyone,' he nods. 'Sorry man, I tried.'

'I know you did and I appreciate it very much.'

'What are your plans now?'

'I might take some time off. I would like to get away from the Valley for a while.'

'Good for you,' Roger sighs. 'How I long for it myself!'

'A vacation you mean?'

'No, for good. Beam me up! I've done enough of these jobs man. They eat into your nerves like termites.'

'I'm surprised,' says Ved. 'Lots of people see you as the quintessential Valley type.'

'Really? In that case, they are looking at a false front. After my kids are through college, my dream is to downsize here and buy a summer home near Tahoe. I hate the liberal politics of the Bay Area anyway. I'll be happy riding my boat, fishing, and maybe teaching in a school, being a role model to some boys or something.'

'Wow, I would never have guessed.'

'Anyway, your timing is good. You're just getting out before the bloodbath begins.'

'I guess so. What's your situation?' Ved asks.

'Looks like I'm done for. My boss too. Once again, politics prevailing over sound business decisions.'

'So for all we know, you too might be a free bird soon.'

'I wish, but I'm not free until my brats are out of college and my Viper is paid for.'

'Well, it was a pleasure working with you, Roger.' They shake hands.

'It was mutual, then,' Roger smiles warmly. 'I will remember you as a good employee and a good man. Enjoy the break and let's stay in touch.'

Ved bids hasty goodbyes to a few more colleagues around his office and sends a short email to many others. He rummages through his business files, papers and books. How easy it is, even pleasurable, to toss this stuff he has held onto for years. He puts a few personal items in a carton to take home. In under an hour, his office is almost as clean as new.

A woman from HR arrives for the exit interview. His paperwork is made easier by his worthless stock options. She clarifies that since he is quitting on his own, he is not eligible for California's unemployment dole. After the formalities, she takes his badge and escorts him out.

He walks for the last time through a space he has inhabited for nearly four years. In the parking lot, he stops for a final, lingering look and then drives away. The end of a chapter. His emotions are mixed. Certainly not an ideal ending, but this Omnicon gig, he decides, was not bad overall. It had its share of drudgery and soul-numbing elements but far less than most jobs people do in the world for far less money. He cannot complain too much.

He reviews his financial situation. The stock market crash has slashed his net worth by half. It is as if his savings for the past six years have been erased. At least he still has his physical and mental health, his mind is frequently lucid, and life still interests him enough. What worries him more is that he is so totally burned out in his profession. What professional and economic road lies ahead of him?

§

Unemployment in Silicon Valley is high. Finding another job will not be easy. In any case, he is in no mood to return to another job right away. Though he must now live on his attenuated savings, it helps that his needs are few and his expenses modest.

The first month after leaving Omnicon goes quickly. He sleeps late and gets up late, surfs the net, and masturbates more often. Porn has to be the killer app on the Internet, he thinks. But who are these people who make so much of it, day after day? They reveal so much hate and self-loathing, so little love and joy. So much of it is cold and callous, rooted in power and domination. Yet porn contains so much more. Its range of sexual morality and politics, he muses, is far more complex than the simplifying narratives that surround it. What exactly is porn doing to his psyche, or to his society? Who can he trust to make sense of all the bizarre games people play with sex?

For meals, he either visits cheap taquerias or fixes up something himself, like tossing a frozen bag of Southwestern style veggies together with chopped onions, green chilies and garam masala, which he eats with pita bread. He eats the coconut curry version with rice. From his local library, he rents nature documentaries and old films by Bergman, Kurosawa, Wenders. He reads *The Brothers Karamazov*. He reads about social contract theory and the State's monopoly on legitimate violence. He enjoys occasional drinks paired with nuts and olives, listens to Fairuz and eats pomegranates. After reading Colin Thubron's *The Lost Heart of Asia*, he toys with the idea of visiting Bukhara and Samarkand. He follows long hiking trails in good weather. At home, he sings old Hindi movie songs and loves it. How he wishes he had a decent voice. Life is simple and pleasurable. For a while, he feels completely self-sufficient.

But this self-sufficiency is short-lived. Before too long, he starts to find his solitude turning into loneliness more often. He begins to crave human company again.

He calls Liz one evening. 'Hello stranger,' he says.

'Hi! I didn't think you would call so soon,' her tone is cordial enough.

'You obviously thought wrong. How's life?'

Almost immediately, she launches into her big news: she has a new lover, an Irishman in real estate. She met him on the same matchmaking website where she met Ved. 'Next month we're flying to Paris for a week, and then spending a weekend in Antwerp, the birthplace of Peter Paul Rubens, an artist James really adores, and I quite like myself.'

Huh, didn't take her long to get over me, he thinks. 'Congratulations. Is he husband material then?'

'Oh, every inch of him. James is so sweet and has this great sense of humour. My friends love him. He is already talking about having me move in with him, into his condo in Sunset.'

'That's great, I'm happy for you. How old is he?'

'He's fifty-nine but looks ten years younger. He still works out every bloody day!'

'Wow, eighteen years older. That must pose some challenges.'

'Nah, not at all,' she asserts. 'Tell me about yourself. What have you been up to?'

'Nothing much. Still trying to figure out what the hell I am doing with my life.'

'Oh, I thought you had it all figured out already, using your superior reason, compassion, and whatnot.' She pauses, then adds with a laugh, 'You know I'm joking, right?'

'Never had a doubt.'

'So, are you any closer to finding someone who doesn't like the "trappings of traditional unions?"' she can barely hide her sarcasm.

'I'm not looking,' he says and tells her about leaving Omnicon. 'I'm just enjoying my solitude right now. Reading lots of books and planning a trip to Central Asia.'

'Sounds adventurous! But wouldn't that be terribly lonely: travelling solo, eating alone in restaurants?'

'Not really. I'm used to it. I tend to talk to the locals more when I travel solo.'

'Well, if and when you get bored with your busy routine, perhaps you can buy me lunch. Oh, did I tell you, I lost 15 pounds from this new diet I'm on? I feel so good!'

§

He calls the district attorney's office to ask about Eddie Morris.

'I am curious,' he asks a junior legal aide. 'What have you learned about his past?'

The aide fetches a dossier and mentions a few details of the kind that go with a driver's licence or a person's public record, including past court cases and misdemeanour rulings, but little that sheds light on Eddie's personal history. 'What about his background: his family, his job, his beliefs, his—'

'An attorney has just been assigned to this case, sir,' the legal aide says. 'He will be adding to this dossier. Rest assured, we will have all the evidence necessary to prosecute the case.'

This is what Ved suspects, that they will proceed with jaded efficiency, and they will seek punishment by the book. But where is the man Eddie in this picture? What is his story?

§

Then one day Ved is taken ill. He has a high fever, chills, bodyaches and diarrhoea. His head pounds, his cough threatens to dismantle his rib cage. Falling in and out of wakefulness, he starts to hallucinate. He knows that this is when it hurts the most; he has no one in his life to even offer him a glass of water, let alone take him to a hospital or cook him a meal. He wonders, if tonight he died in his apartment, how long would it be before someone found out? At some point, after his calls go unanswered, the apartment manager would come knocking for the rent. Or a neighbour might complain of the stench from his maggot-infested body.

In his feverish delirium, even his suffering feels voluptuous. He remembers his time with Pooja in Cairo, when they both came down with high fevers, and spent two whole days in a hotel room, clinging to each other in bed, flesh burning against flesh. How Pooja had woken up screaming from a nightmare in which Ved had been transformed into a desiccated mummy, like the ones they'd seen at the Egyptian national museum. This and other memories start to trickle in and soon become a deluge.

Hardly ever in their two years did he look into her eyes and tell her that he loved her, even when things were going well. All at once, he can see that he was too miserly in love, even pitiless. Too self-absorbed. How could she have been happy with him? A gnawing remorse envelops him now, for which he fears he can find no atonement.

Drenched in sweat, he lies awake late into the night, tossing and turning, fighting back tears. It strikes him that his idea of love may well be more theoretical than real. Perhaps he has always been afraid to succumb to its calling. To succumb to it, he can now see, is to be openly and honestly vulnerable—to see himself as an ordinary man with his share of frailties. Liz was mostly right in her diagnosis, after all. Can he change now, or is he too set in his ways? Try to change he must, he quietly resolves. This is no good way to live a life.

§

Ved is mostly recovered in three days and though still weak, he ventures out for a walk. He calls Ravi from a park bench. They brief each other on the salient events in their lives. Ravi's upbeat mood makes Ved postpone the news of his assault. Ravi relishes every bit of woe that has descended on Omnicon. He reveals that he now works for a company that sells 'direct email marketing solutions.'

'Sounds like spam!' Ved exclaims.

'That's one perspective. We think email is a powerful way to connect buyers and sellers.'

'C'mon man, are you serious? What are they mixing in your water in that office?'

'Relax,' Ravi chuckles, 'I'm kidding. I know it's spam. Remember I needed a job to stay in the US? This is the best I could find. An Indian guy runs this company. The bugger saw my desperation and took me on for peanuts. I'm biding my time; my job search continues.'

'Ah, that explains it. I was getting worried. How is Kavita?'

'She's good. She might get a real job soon, one with a normal engineer's salary.'

'Great, let's meet for lunch one of these days. In fact, bring her along.'

'Sure, but I'm busy the next couple of weeks and then we're off to Florida for a week. Vacation, you know. Kavita has been pestering me; all her friends have been there. Orlando and all. Let's shoot for next month. I'll call you.'

§

At his local public library one day, Ved sees a listing for a part-time job—shelving books mainly, but also helping people find what they are looking for. The job appeals to him at once. He imagines a therapeutic, meditative quality in it. Buddhist monks making sand mandalas come to mind. Why not try it out for a while? It'll also keep him plugged into people, the one part of his last job he misses. Who knows, the thought crosses his mind, he might even meet an interesting woman. The idea tickles him.

He applies for the job. After a short and candid

interview, he is hired and starts spending his afternoons at the library. It is nothing like making sand mandalas but he is satisfied with the simple routine it provides him. He enjoys browsing new releases and discovering old titles of books, films and music. He meets people from many walks of life.

His college friends call when they learn that he has quit his job. 'What?' Balaji cannot hide his patronizing tone, 'You are doing a clerical job in a public library? Do you want me to call around for a real job?' He is mystified when Ved tells him that he's doing this for his mental health. Balaji probes further but remains sceptical. 'Whatever dude,' he finally lets out a chuckle, 'Let me know when you change your mind. What are friends for?'

One day Ved comes across an anonymous quote on a web forum: 'Intimacy with anyone with flaws requires us to be mindful and compassionate towards our own flaws. We often say that love is elusive. It is not. Love is omnipresent. It asks us to be better people. And often we simply refuse.' He prints the quote in large font and tapes it on a wall in his kitchen.

§

There is a knock on his door one morning. Through the peephole, he sees a petite white woman who, when he opens the door, introduces herself as a Jehovah's Witness. He has read about Jehovah's Witnesses and their evangelism but has never met one. Realizing he is Indian, she says, 'Years ago, my mother spent a whole year in India as a missionary. She brought back the most amazing stories! I too would love to follow in her footsteps.'

Pleasantries over, she begins her spiel, 'Don't you think, sir, that there is too much pain and suffering in the world today?' Ved leans against the doorframe and nods. She continues, 'Don't you think our world is brimming with cruelty and hatred? Like me, I bet you're worried about what you can do to make the world a better place.' He nods again. She hasn't said anything objectionable yet, so he keeps listening.

'People are hurting too much to think things through,' she continues, her eyes aglow with conviction, 'so they cause more pain to themselves and to others. Job put it well: "Man, born of woman, is short-lived and glutted with agitation." Fortunately, the Bible shows us the way—it promises a new world, where righteousness will prevail. But before the ideal conditions that the Bible prophesies are realized, mankind must go through a time of unprecedented wickedness. Then, as Matthew said, "He that has endured to the end is the one that will be saved."'

She pulls out a booklet and searches for a page, 'Here it is. This psalm describes what the Messianic King will do for mankind.'

She may be living proof of humankind's ancient search for meaning in life, but he decides he has no time for her stupid crap. He longs to be rid of her. 'Listen, you are wasting your time. I am not interested. Thank you.'

'Sir, can I ask you why? Do you not desire the fulfillment of God's promises for us?'

'What promises? This Messianic King of yours is an illusion, a false hope. God died a long time ago for me—a joyous event in my life. I don't miss him, nor want him back.'

Her face remains calm, the kind of calm that, he suspects, only comes from insufficient doubt and plentiful ignorance. She tries again but Ved holds his ground. She thanks him for his time and leaves. Seconds later he hears her knock on his neighbour's door.

His tolerance for evangelists of all stripes—religious and secular—has diminished over the years. People like her, he reflects, and that other set of secular fundamentalists in America, with their faith in free markets and techno-utopianism, are, in fact, siblings under the skin, both afraid to look squarely at the darkly irrational and unstable human substrate. Both disregard the evidence that does not suit their purposes. They implicitly believe that history has a design, that it can converge to a universal civilization where people would come to acquire the same values, that only false beliefs obstruct the path to the perfect society. He wonders: What if this woman realized in old age that her core beliefs were a pack of lies? Some dislocation that would be!

He too has struggled against his own lies and confusions—about his social identity, meaning, purpose—and absorbed its dislocations. In moments of lucidity, he sees his life for the stage play it is. He sees, too, that there is no stepping off his stage and out of the play. Trapped therein, he longs to perform with a measure of dignity and grace.

Where to find dignity and grace? The most promising lead he has is to make room for love in his life. Not a sappy, feel-good, or needy kind of love, nor mere romantic love, but a love that fuels living with an open heart, free from pride and resentment, with an alert compassion for all. He is alone in his balcony in the quiet of the night. Without warning, his eyes mist over. He is suddenly overwhelmed with feeling. It is like the promise of a whole new beginning.

Fifteen

VED'S PHONE RINGS ONE MORNING.

'Bhaiya-ji,' he hears a soft voice speaking Hindi with a Punjabi accent, 'I am Rashmi. Wife of Baldev. We talked in the store last month.'

'Yes, yes, I remember. How are you?' he leans forward, bracing for bad news.

'Can you help me please?' she says in a pleading voice.

'Yes, of course. Are you okay? What kind of help do you want?'

'I want to leave my husband. Today. As soon as possible. I cannot take it anymore. You said you know a women's organization that can help me.'

'Yes. I can take you there. Where are you now?'

'I'm at home. My husband is not here. He is working at the store.'

Ved takes down her address. 'I'll pick you up in an hour. Be sure to pack all your personal documents and other valuables. I'll call you when I'm on your street.'

Before he has time to work it all out, he calls in sick at the library, locates Rashmi's street on his map of Oakland, and leaves. He carries a baseball cap that he will put on near her apartment to partially cover his face. On the drive, he wonders what might have compelled Rashmi to call him. A part of him dreads getting entangled in a truly messy situation. Another part wants to do the right thing, to help this woman. He fears that if he turns away now, it would haunt him for a long time.

However, doubts flare up again. Maybe he should give Rashmi the phone number for Saheli, the local organization that helps South Asian victims of domestic abuse, and ask her to call them directly? Aren't they far better equipped to handle such cases? He doesn't even know where they are located. He finally decides that since time may not be on her side, he will pick her up, bring her to his place, and then contact Saheli.

Rashmi's street is in a working-class neighbourhood with a string of two and three-storey apartment complexes. Plastic bags and other dry refuse lie scattered in some of the parking lots. He hears his mother's voice in his head, *Arre, look! Just like India!* He can see no one around her apartment building. He parks directly in front and calls Rashmi.

Rashmi promptly comes down the stairs with one duffle bag and then goes up again for a suitcase. Anita follows behind with a small pack of her own. Ved loads their luggage into the trunk. Beneath Rashmi's salwar-kameez, she clearly looks pregnant this time. Within seconds, without any pleasantries, they are all in his car, driving back to San Francisco. He turns to look at Rashmi and notices tears rolling down her cheeks. There is a fresh bruise on her chin.

'Are you both physically okay?' he asks Rashmi, who nods. 'Please don't worry, you are safe now.' Her sniffling reduces somewhat. After a short pause, he asks, 'Did you tell anyone where you were going?'

She shakes her head. 'But I left a note for him...saying that I am leaving him.' While she uses a combination of Hindi, Punjabi and English, he uses Hindi and English.

'After your call, I didn't have time to contact Saheli,' he tells her. 'We can do that when we reach my apartment. Okay?' She nods.

'Are you hungry?' he asks. She says no. To dispel the gloomy silence, Ved turns on the radio. A story about the intensifying ground combat in Fallujah is on NPR; scores of people have died. When they reach Ved's place, he leaves her luggage in the car and takes them up.

'Have your parents gone back home?' she asks inside the apartment.

'Yes.'

He realizes she would have felt more at ease with them around, rather than being with a single man in his apartment. He brings them water. Rashmi slumps heavily onto the futon sofa and breaks down into tears. Perhaps the enormity of her step has dawned on her afresh. Anita stands against the wall, staring at her mother through large, expressive eyes. Her hair is unkempt and one of her shoelaces has come undone.

'I feel so ashamed telling you this,' Rashmi begins in a feeble voice. 'It was one thing for me to bear his physical and verbal abuses. I kept praying to Guru Sahib to change his heart. But a few months ago, he began to stay out longer. New smells came from his clothes. My fears were confirmed when I awoke one night and noticed him on the phone, talking and acting dirty. I realized that he had befriended a dissolute woman, a prostitute, because no respectable woman talks to someone like that.

'And last night something happened that drove me over the edge,' Rashmi says. 'He brought this other woman home! He locked me and Anita in the bedroom, while he and that woman drank and did filthy things to each other in the living room.' Rashmi starts to sob. 'That was so humiliating! I sat there in total shock. I finally accepted that I was nothing more than a naukrani to him.'

Fresh tears roll down her cheeks. This morning, when she gathered all her courage and confronted Baldev, he hit her repeatedly, calling her a rundee, a whore. She reveals that she is five months pregnant. She was afraid and didn't know who else to call. She knows no one in her neighbourhood. She didn't want to call the police either, because she has seen the 'kallu' policemen of Oakland and she is afraid of them. Her casual prejudice bothers Ved but he lets it pass. Why hold it against her when even his cosmopolitan college friends often refer to black people that way.

Ved assures Rashmi that she did the right thing by contacting him. 'What will Baldev do when he finds your note?' he asks. She shrugs. Ved thinks it unlikely that Baldev will contact the police. If they find her, that will only land him in trouble. 'What if,' asks Ved, 'Baldev came and apologized to you profusely in a few days? Can you imagine patching things up with him?'

'Nahin,' she says firmly, wiping her cheek, a new resolve shining in her eyes. 'I cannot live with that vile man. What if he hurt the baby next time?' she instinctively draws her hand to her belly. 'I will not go back to him unless Guru Sahibji makes him undergo a genuine change of heart,' she gestures at the ceiling.

Ved looks up the number for Saheli's hotline and dials with the speakerphone on. A woman volunteer answers in English. Ved invites Rashmi to speak to her directly but Rashmi chokes up, so Ved summarizes what he knows about her case to the volunteer, and how he himself got involved.

'I'm so glad that Rashmi and her child are not in imminent danger,' the woman says. She then explains Saheli's services. They can pair up Rashmi with a Punjabi-speaking counsellor, who will help her find a temporary shelter, since their own small shelter for Indian women is full. Rashmi will likely be referred to a shelter run by the State of California that's open to all women. Besides food and basic living expenses, Saheli can provide grants and loans to file criminal charges, pursue litigation or resolve immigration issues. Above all, Saheli helps women get back on their feet and support themselves. Rashmi listens carefully.

The volunteer arranges a meeting between Rashmi and the counsellor for the next day. Meanwhile, if Rashmi needs a place to stay, she should call a California State shelter right away. The volunteer provides a number for their area. She also provides the name and number of the counsellor who will meet Rashmi. Ved and Rashmi thank the woman and end the call.

Ved discusses the call with Rashmi to ensure she has understood what the volunteer said. He suspects that he and Rashmi are both thinking the same thing, so he broaches the topic. 'What do you want to do now? You can stay here tonight if you wish—if you feel comfortable. I have a guest room back there. Or I can call this shelter for you and take you there. It's up to you.'

She looks torn. 'I don't want to be a burden on you, bhaiya-ji,' she says after a few seconds. 'But if it is okay with you, can I stay here for one night?'

'Of course, it's no problem for me. It might be easier too; the counsellor can just meet you here tomorrow.' He fetches their luggage from the garage, shows them into the guest bedroom, and encourages Rashmi to rest for a while. 'If you have any more questions for Saheli, you can call them again,' Ved says, pointing at the phone in the room. Before stepping out, he gives her the piece of paper with Saheli's hotline number on it, and gently closes the door behind him.

When Rashmi emerges a couple of hours later, Ved makes tea for both of them. They sit around the dining table with tea and namkeen. 'The counsellor will likely ask what you want to do,' Ved says. 'Whether you want to stay in this country or return to India.'

'India,' Rashmi says without hesitation. 'I don't have any family or friends here. How can I live on my own in my condition? It is best that I go back to my parents.'

'The counsellor will also ask if you want to file criminal charges against Baldev.'

'I don't want the police involved,' Rashmi says firmly. 'I know Guru Sahibji will punish him in His own way.'

They drink and eat for a while in silence until Rashmi begins to talk. Her openness, her trust in him, strikes Ved as endearing. He learns that in Rashmi's eighteen months in the US, Baldev hasn't even set her up with a bank account or a credit card, nor taught her how to drive a car. Her spousal visa does not allow her to work in the US. With her pregnancy, there is little chance she can survive here on her own. Going back to her parents is probably her only option. If Bollywood created a villain based on Baldev, Ved thinks, many people might see a caricature in it. Reality can so often seem nastier than what we are willing to consider plausible in fiction. An image of Eddie comes to his mind. What of him? he wonders. An incorrigible criminal and low life, or a caricature?

'How will your parents react when they find out?' Ved asks.

'They will be devastated,' Rashmi says sadly. 'My father will feel very guilty because when I first met Baldev, I didn't like him. There was something about him...his eyes? His swagger? ...I didn't trust him. My father cajoled me into it; he said I was imagining things. One of my aunts even sneered at me: "You are just a plain, ordinary girl, not some apsara. You think you can land a better boy than him? He comes from a good family. He even lives in Am-reeka!"'

Rashmi's story puts Ved in a sombre mood. She will likely also face victim-blaming at home, including from this aunt. Ved suggests a simple, early dinner: alu-gobi, dal, rice. Rashmi agrees, rising to prepare the food. But Ved insists that he will manage by himself in the kitchen; better she look after Anita, who seems afraid and confused.

He leaves the TV on while he cooks. The evening news has more coverage of the war, reeking with lies, bluster and chauvinism; American deaths get mourned far more than Iraqi ones. When not preoccupied with Anita, Rashmi gazes at the screen absently.

She eats quietly while also feeding Anita, who, for

a three-year-old, has been unusually subdued all day, despite Ved's attempts to cheer her up with kiddie-talk. It is as if a shadow of fear surrounds her too, as if her mother's sorrow has infected her. It occurs to Ved that Pooja's daughter must be the same age as Anita. Is she shy or a chirpy kid?

'Thank you for your kindness, bhaiya-ji,' Rashmi says after dinner, her eyes teary again. She soon retires to her room with Anita and locks the door. Ved wonders if this is the first time she has spent a night under the same roof with an unrelated man.

§

The counsellor arrives at eleven the next morning. Ved leaves her with Rashmi in the living room and retreats to his own bedroom. An hour later, the counsellor is ready to go. Ved walks out with her to her car. 'What do you think?' he asks.

'Gosh, such a tragic case. I think she has very few options left. In her place, I would return to India, too. I usually recommend a cooling-off period, but I'm not so sure that would be a good idea in this case. Her husband seems to be near the psychopathic end of the spectrum.'

'Can Saheli host Rashmi and Anita for a few days, until they go? They also need money for their flights back home.'

'As I told Rashmi, she can either stay at a California State shelter or with the family of one of our volunteers from the Indian community. I think the family option will be better for her. I will put out a call in the next hour and let her know. Our funds are tight but let me see what we can do for the flights. We usually offer loans but we should be able to chip in something.' Hours later she calls Rashmi to say that a Bengali couple in San Jose, and a family in Fremont, a Tamilian couple with two kids, are willing to host her.

'You have a third option too,' Ved tells Rashmi. 'You are welcome to just stay here till your departure, unless you prefer to stay with a family.'

'I don't know,' Rashmi is torn. 'I don't know these people; who knows how they will turn out? But I also don't want to be a burden on you, bhaiya-ji.'

Over dinner, they talk and she decides to stay at Ved's place until her departure, hopefully within a few days.

After dinner, Rashmi goes to her room and breaks the news to her family in India. When she emerges again, she tearfully recounts the shock and horror it provoked in her family. She heard a lot of commotion in the background of the call and suspects that her mother might even have fainted. Her father wants her to come back as soon as possible.

§

It has been four days since Rashmi and Anita arrived in his apartment. Not only has he adjusted to their presence, he does not resent them for squeezing his space and privacy. This is unlike him and it surprises Ved. It helps that he spends his afternoons working in the library, from where he has also borrowed some puzzles and picture books for Anita.

To feel more useful, Rashmi has started cooking one meal a day. Though he finds her cooking scarcely better than his own, her repertoire is both different and more authentic, whereas he learned to cook in America out of necessity, relying on fusion and experiment.

He has called an Indian travel agent. Due to the high season, the cheaper flights were all sold out for two weeks. The agent put them on a waitlist. Rashmi only has a few dollars with her—that along with her marriage jewels constitute her net worth. Saheli has offered only $400, so Ved decides to pay the balance for their tickets. Rashmi says she will have her father pay him back but, in his mind, Ved has already written off the money. It's money well spent, he thinks.

Rashmi tells Ved about the conflict that has erupted between Baldev's and Rashmi's families back home. Her family had hoped that Baldev's family would be upset by their son's behaviour and would try to bring him to his senses, but when his parents blamed Rashmi for the situation, her father stormed out, demanding that Baldev's family pay back the large dowry they took. Baldev, it seems clear, has shown little remorse over his conduct, nor expressed a desire to have Rashmi and Anita back. It's safe to assume that he has not filed a police case.

Returning from the library one evening, Ved walks past Baldev's store and peers inside. There he is, handling a customer from behind the counter. What if he finds out that his wife has taken refuge in Ved's apartment, only two blocks away? It could turn messy. Rashmi too is aware of the risk and never goes on the front balcony or leaves the apartment.

Though still downbeat, Rashmi is beginning to show an interest in the world beyond her marriage. She timidly asks how Ved came to the US, what he does for a living. But it is hard for her to relate to his station in life, partly because they represent different classes of Indians in America. She asks about the recent cuts on his face. Ved tells her the story of his assault.

'Too many bad men in the world,' she says to commiserate.

'I want to know what this man is like, what fuels his rage,' he says.

While he reads after dinner, she shuffles through the channels on TV, pausing longest on the hokiest soaps and sitcoms. At other times, she lets Anita watch cartoons. She once expressed awe at his bookshelves. 'So many books!' she exclaimed. She picked up a book one day and asked, 'Gogol? What kind of a name is Gogol? Too much reading, baba. Your job must be hard.'

'These are unrelated to my job,' he explained. 'I read them for fun.'

A bewildered look crossed her face, 'These are storybooks?'

'Some are,' he paused briefly. 'Well, in a way they all are. Yes, strictly speaking, they are all just storybooks, every one of them,' his knowing half-smile lost on her.

Anita too has grown more accustomed to her temporary home. Often when he returns from the library, he finds her toys scattered across the living room floor. She has even begun to chuckle and respond to Ved more readily.

Rashmi bathes after cooking each morning, puts on a fresh salwar-kameez, and steps out on an interior corridor to dry her long and lustrous black hair in the sun. Not so long ago, with her glow of youth and innocence, she too must have quickened the heartbeats of young men in her neighbourhood. She holds a BA in Home Science from Punjab University. She says she was a good badminton player too, an image Ved finds hard to reconcile with her present lot: 30–40 pounds heavier, harried and joyless, facing a bleak future as a single mother in Punjab.

On Sunday, Ved smuggles out Rashmi and Anita in his car. Halfway across town, he stops and buys them lunch at a coffee shop that he and Pooja had often visited on weekends. He gets his old favourite, the grilled cheese and mushroom sandwich. Afterwards, he takes them to Golden Gate Park. A jazz concert is on; hundreds of people are stretched out on the lawns. They too sit and listen. Rashmi, looking self-conscious in her silken green salwar-kameez, has never been to a concert in the US, and watches the spectacle with utmost fascination. They both keep an eye on Anita who has found two playmates nearby.

The next day the travel agent offers two seats on a flight in two weeks at an acceptable price. The same day, after checking with Rashmi, Ved pays for their tickets. By her departure date, she would have stayed with him for about twenty days.

Sixteen

VED GETS A NOTICE FROM the district attorney's office. He must appear before a judge next week to testify at a preliminary hearing. Given the hate crime dimension in his case, Eddie Morris will likely be tried for a felony rather than a misdemeanour.

Eddie has been on his mind for weeks. What is the man like? How does he think? What has made him so angry and afraid? Does he now regret his act of violence? Just how far gone is he? All Ved knows from the attorney's office is that he is an auto mechanic and has a mother and two siblings in Arizona. Ved wants to know more about him before the testimony, or else he may end up aiding the cause of punishment rather than of justice.

Ved gets up early on Tuesday and tells Rashmi, 'I have some unfinished business with a man named Edward Morris. I should be back within eight hours.' He adds with a smile, 'If you don't hear from me by then, follow the instructions in the envelope on my table.' She returns a mildly alarmed look and nods, but says nothing.

He had spotted Eddie's address on a document at the district attorney's office. He expects the drive to take just over two hours. Traffic is light and the weather pleasant. He is tense but not afraid. He plays out various scenarios for the encounter in his head. He must first be certain that Eddie is sober when they meet; if not, he will abort his mission and walk away. He must remain calm and focus on his goal, which is to try and assess for himself whether Eddie, and society at large, will be served better by keeping Eddie in jail for two–three years. Ved has long disliked the overly retributive prison system in America, with its lack of focus on reform. Private prisons have made things worse, creating incentives to incarcerate more people. What if Eddie needs help, not isolation behind bars? In that case, wouldn't mercy, perhaps alongside counselling, be a better stimulus for reform?

On a whim, Ved stops at a farm outlet along the highway to pick up two baskets of strawberries. Getting off the highway, he easily locates Eddie's address: a modest apartment block sandwiched between a gas station and a motel. He parks along the curb, climbs a flight of steps, walks down a corridor, and reaches Eddie's door. There is not a soul in sight. Suddenly a flush of anxiety courses through him. Is he about to make a huge mistake? He struggles to keep his composure. He focuses his thoughts, takes a deep breath, and knocks.

The door opens within seconds. There he is. The man who assaulted him.

Ved steps back instinctively. Eddie, in dark jeans and white T-shirt, squints at him. He has a pale two-day stubble, but does not appear intoxicated.

'Hi, my name is Ved. We met at that gas station.'

A sudden look of recognition crosses Eddie's face. He is visibly baffled and looks around to see if Ved has company.

'I'm alone. I came to meet you.'

'Why?' Eddie asks sharply, looking even more baffled, 'What do you want from me?'

'Nothing. I just want to talk for a few minutes, if you would please allow me,' Ved requests with folded hands.

'Fuck! I don't believe this.' Eddie says and bangs the door shut.

'Eddie, wait!' Ved knocks again.

'Go away,' Eddie hollers. 'There is nothing to talk about, you...'

Ved thinks he heard the word 'scum' but he can't be sure. What should he do now? He stands there frozen, his trip threatening to be in vain. He knocks again, amazed at his own nerve and persistence. 'This is about next week. It won't take long.'

After what seems like an eternity, the door opens.

'Listen, I know you are spooked by my appearance here. Let me just say that I don't hate you for what you did to me, and I am not angling for revenge. I just came to talk, okay?'

'Talk about what?' Eddie asks, standing in the doorway, looking stern and crabby.

'This won't take long, I promise. Can I talk to you out here for a few minutes?' Eddie considers it, then steps out in the corridor, leaving his door open.

Ved steals a glance at the living room floor strewn with shoes and clothes, dishes on the coffee table, cheap furniture. A mounted US flag hangs at one end of the living room. His dirty blonde hair covers his earlobes but not what appears to be a birthmark beneath his left ear—a nickel-sized blotch of purple skin. A shiny dark scorpion is tattooed on his right forearm.

'You like strawberries?' Ved blurts out nervously.

Their eyes meet. Ved manages to hold his stare until Eddie averts his eyes to look at the bag with suspicion. 'I got some for you, very fresh.'

When Eddie does not take it, Ved sets the bag down by the door, his peripheral vision watching the distance between himself and the tall, burly Eddie. He notices a poster inside the apartment displaying three rows of handgun models below the words *Celebrate Diversity* in rainbow colours.

'Sorry to bug you, but I had to meet you again,' Ved forces an awkward half-smile, 'under different circumstances.'

'We'll meet in court,' Eddie mutters. 'Settle the score then.' He leans against the wall by the door, his legs spread, still looking baffled. His head is cocked defiantly but his voice sounds defeated. Perhaps his latest brushes with law enforcement agencies have cowed him down a bit.

'About that court hearing next week, I heard you'll be tried for a felony this time, and will probably get two–three years in jail.' Eddie's face betrays no emotion. Ved continues, 'That'll be no fun. When you come out, you won't easily find a job, or a girlfriend.'

'What do you want from me?' Eddie asks brusquely. 'Who sent you here?'

'I came on my own. Ever since that night, I've wondered about you.'

Eddie remains silent yet suspicious. 'Listen,' Ved speaks in a calm, deliberate voice. 'I hope you don't have to go to prison. I'm willing to ask for leniency in my testimony next week.'

Eddie's eyes squint into a confused look. 'Why?' he asks. 'What game are you playing with me?'

'It's simple: Help me understand why you assaulted me, and I might help you avoid prison.'

'Why? Why would you help me?'

'Look, I don't want prison to do its worst to you. Prison will fuck you up. If I think you deserve another chance, I'll help you. In your place, I know I'd like that chance.' Ved resumes after a pause, 'Just help me understand why you attacked me. What were you thinking?'

Eddie has a faraway look. His arms have slackened, his shoulders droop. 'I was upset. A lot of shit is goin' on against this country. And people like Johnny are havin' to pay for it.'

'What do you mean? Who is Johnny?'

'My brother. Johnny.' Eddie breathes in deep, stares out in the distance for a few seconds, then says, 'He got his legs blown off in the war.'

The violence in his description jolts Ved, 'Jeez! How did that happen?'

'IED. His vehicle got hit by a roadside bomb.' Eddie's brow is dense with furrows.

'Oh, man. I'm sorry to hear that.' The air crackles with tension, and now Eddie has an Arab at his doorstep, or so he must think. No need to disabuse him, let him discover on his own.

'Where is Johnny now?'

'Rehab.'

'That's very tragic. Must have been really hard on your family. But tell me then, why did you punch *me*, of all people? Why not punch the politicians who sent your brother to war?'

Not that Ved was expecting a brilliant response from Eddie but all he gets is scowls and mutters, 'They attacked us...Johnny fought for our country...against evil... defending our freedom...they hate our values.' Looking agitated, Eddie shrinks into the doorframe.

'What are your values?' Ved asks but Eddie does not respond.

A pathetic man. Not an iota of good sense in him, thinks Ved. No doubt he buys into all the bullshit about America's special mission in the world, that it only fights necessary wars, that it is a force of freedom against tyranny, good against evil. Ved wonders how Eddie could ever peer through the fog of jingoism to see America as just another empire with both its effulgence and its dark side. Or as a land of corporations, whose self-interest lies in making the world safe for capitalism by hook or by crook. Could he ever see that men like his brother are nothing but cannon fodder in this great game? Or how moribund the American Dream is, that people of his class will likely remain where they are? Or that if Jesus came back to earth and visited America, he might be shocked to see what so many of his followers do in his name?

'Ok, so hitting me was your way of defending your values and freedom? Tell me how that works.' A sense of power courses through Ved. His voice exudes command. 'And what did Johnny think of what you did to me? Was he proud of you?'

'Don't fuckin' preach to me,' Eddie mutters angrily, though he hangs his head. 'I don't take shit from nobody.'

'You're angry, eh!' Ved stares at him. 'Like that other night, when you beat me up and made America proud?'

'That's enough shit!' Eddie raises his voice; his eyes glowering. 'Is this why you came here? To fuckin' lecture me?'

Ved lowers his voice, speaks slowly. 'I came here to find out why you hit me the other night. Why? Why, goddammit?'

'All right!' Eddie hollers. 'I was burning up. I got carried away. I screwed up, okay?'

Ved takes that in. 'You screwed up big time. Does that mean you regret it?'

'I shouldn't have done that,' Eddie says, without looking at Ved, his voice entering a lower register. 'I got nothing against you. I was drinking and shit. I got carried away.'

At last, a concession of sorts, thinks Ved. Not an apology but a step in the right direction.

'Now leave.' Eddie's voice is no longer menacing; it is almost like a loud appeal.

'Fine, I'll leave now,' Ved says. He decides right then that he will help Eddie. At times, wrote Marcus Aurelius, 'The best revenge is to be unlike him who performed the injury.' Eddie may be an idiot but he is not too far gone, not enough to be locked up for two–three years. Ved decides to make a leniency plea for Eddie next week. That will give this foolish fucker something to think about.

'All right, Eddie, I'll help you avoid prison. How does that sound?'

Eddie turns to meet his eyes. He wants to speak but the words do not come. He averts his eyes, then looks at Ved again.

'Thanks for your time,' Ved says, 'See you next week.'

Ved extends his hand out to Eddie who hesitates at first, then shakes it.

'Thanks,' Eddie says weakly. His palm is coarse.

Ved turns and walks down the stairs.

§

The confrontation with Eddie went far better than he had expected, Ved reflects on his drive home. He is glad he went. He even feels a sense of closure, with a way of framing and overcoming this ugly episode. Of course, what happens after his testimony and leniency plea next week will be between Eddie and the people of the State of California—that part is beyond his control.

It also strikes Ved that most of the people he knows would probably call him crazy for helping Eddie. A mushy fool, they will say. Ved's parents too; he had better cook up some story for them.

Seventeen

THE FOLLOWING DAY, IT OCCURS to Ved that perhaps this would be the perfect time for him to go to India for an extended stay, maybe for a year. The American job market is bleak, and he is so burned-out anyway. What has he got to lose? He is in between jobs. What better time than now?

If India has changed, he has changed even more. His desire to reconnect with it has only grown over the years. He will now see new things—or old things afresh—and make new mental connections, which may well get him out of the funk he is in. He recalls Mark Twain: 'Twenty years from now you will be more disappointed by the things you didn't do than by the ones you did. So throw off the bowlines. Sail away from the safe harbor. Catch the trade winds in your sails. Explore. Dream.'

The idea grips him powerfully. He thinks about it non-stop. What a great chance this is to visit the places he has dreamed of for years: Ladakh, Sikkim, Goa, Assam, Orissa! To wander the ruins of lost cities, trek to Gangotri, read Kabir in Kashi! It will certainly cost him a lot less than simply staying put in San Francisco. It might even revitalize him for his next job. Or perhaps uncover a new vocation. There is only one way to find out. He mentally scans the logistics of the move and finds nothing too daunting. He can make it happen in a couple of weeks, perhaps even by the time of Rashmi's departure.

Dissenting voices arise too: what will he do about sex during his year in India, where it'll be even harder to find a lover. But sexual mores are said to be loosening in India, so that part may well turn out to be a fruitful adventure. On the whole, he finds the pros of an extended trip to India vastly outweighing the cons. If things don't turn out well, he can always return sooner. After three days of constant deliberation, he decides to go for it.

He calls his parents. They still think he is at Omnicon, so he tells them that he is quitting his job to come to India for a year. 'They value my work so much that when I return, they will hire me back,' he lies to soothe their nerves.

But they are plainly alarmed by his decision—the idea of choosing to go without work for a year is utterly alien to them. No one they know has done anything this reckless. 'This is the time to be working hard and rising in your career...like your friends are doing,' Father says. Only the thought of him being closer to them mitigates their protests.

With the decision made, he starts rolling with the preparations. He announces the decision in an email to his friends and acquaintances. He calls the travel agent and is able to get a seat on the same flight as Rashmi and Anita. Rashmi is thrilled by this development—she will have help negotiating international airports with a child. Upon arrival, they decide, she should exit the airport separately from him, lest her family get funny ideas. Right now, they think Rashmi is staying with an Indian couple, not with a single man. Better that they hear the story from her.

He gives notice to his landlord and library, moves all his bank and credit card accounts online, and rents a storage space for furniture, books, utensils, wall décor, and other household items. Sunil offers to look after his car—his stay-at-home wife can use it. At their behest, Ved instructs the post office to forward his mail to them. With each passing day, he feels more and more free, with rising anticipation for the year ahead.

In recent weeks, he has made multiple visits to the dental surgeon, and things have gone according to plan. He will be 'all repaired' after his upcoming last visit, says the surgeon. He has even fixed up Ved's troublesome old molar with a root canal. At Eddie's court hearing, Ved's appeal for clemency is met with disbelief, though Eddie's eyes suggest he is grateful for it.

§

Liz calls, responding to his email. 'I'm so happy for you, and a tad jealous.' They chat for a while about dates and logistics, then wish each other well.

Vikram hosts a going-away dinner for him at home. Balaji and Sunil attend with their wives. 'Here is to Ved having a great time in India,' Balaji raises a toast. 'So what exactly do you plan on doing there?'

'The plan is simple: read and travel, hear lots of stories, understand how India is changing, eat mangoes, jamuns and local foods. Above all, have a jolly good time.'

'Wow, I wish I could do that too,' Balaji says wistfully.

'I have no desire to do that,' Parvathy, Balaji's wife,

interjects. She cites a wealthy Indian-American couple who moved back to Bangalore with their pre-teen kids, lived in a posh gated community, had a Mercedes Benz with a chauffeur, and first-world comforts at home. But they got tired of it in eighteen months and returned. Too much hassle, the woman said. 'She had a point, you know,' added Parvathy. 'Life was hard, managing all their servants was a big task in itself. She realized that she now saw India quite differently. The place had lost its charm for her; it now mostly irritated her—its noise, trash, crowds, the stench of urine in city streets, the madcap traffic, sexism, corruption. Then there was the poor road, water, and electric infrastructure. She just didn't see enough positives to compensate for the negatives. She began to miss her life in Fremont, concluding that contrary to how some Indians think, America was a much better place to raise her two daughters.' More stories are shared of Indian-Americans who went back home but returned within a couple of years.

'I can deal with the chaos,' Balaji says, 'but it jars my nerves to see how cheap life is in India. With all that desperate, in-your-face poverty, I think living a first-world lifestyle in India would grate more on my conscience. Not sure I want to fight that battle.'

'You know,' Balaji continues, 'it's funny how Indians, despite their obsessive adherence to the rules of religion and tradition, abandon all rules and order in public life. Look at their shocking lack of civic sense—how they drive, jump queues, and sneak past all manner of sensible regulations.'

'Yeah,' Vikram chimes in, 'I can only take Indian cities

in small doses. But the truth is that there are now fewer reasons to miss India: we get practically everything from home out here. Roohafza, Lijjat papad, Gongura pickle, even jalebis and cham cham.'

Chuckles fill the air as more products are mentioned. Vikram continues, 'So the only reason to live in India now is to care for our parents in old age. We think, though, that it's a lot easier to just bring them here. That way they can also benefit from the hi-tech healthcare in this country.' All of a piece, Ved thinks; Vikram downplaying the disruption in the parents' lives, his distaste for the actual grimy India, and his feel-good fantasies of 'Hindu civilization'.

Vikram's wife, Nandita, nodding in agreement, adds, 'Another big problem with returning now is that our kids, though only seven and nine, are already too American. It'll be hard for them to adjust. I asked myself: what right do we have to uproot them now?'

'India has a very different sense of privacy and personal space,' says Balaji. 'I predict that the American in you will want to come back after your honeymoon is over.'

'Keep your sense of humour about all the corruption and red tape,' advises Sunil. Vikram follows up with a joke about Indian bureaucracy that evokes further chuckles. Balaji shudders at his memory of the sticky heat in Madras, and the diarrhoea he got there on his last visit. He exhorts Ved to get all the vaccinations he can before leaving.

'Tell me something,' says Balaji, 'did that assault have anything to do with your decision to go to India for so long? Did it alter your feelings for America?'

An uneasy silence. Ved notices all eyes glued on him.

'No, not really. Not in any conscious way. My idea of America—and surely yours too—is based on a much wider set of experiences. One bad trip can't alter it much, at least not something so random like this. If I let that happen, it would dishonour my memory of so many positive experiences. Truth is that I've wanted to spend time in India for years, and this is as good a time as any. I've talked about it earlier, though you didn't believe me then.'

Yet, on the way back to his apartment, Ved wonders if the assault reinforced what he has long felt in his bones. Even if he became a US citizen and lived here for decades, would the world grant him his full claim on America, or readily admit him into blood-and-soil descriptors like 'being American'? In some ways, he will always remain an outsider. The trick, he now thinks, is to see this not as a bane but a blessing—of feeling enough at home in both India and the US, yet also enough of an outsider—an undervalued aspect of intellectual freedom in our age.

He knows India will throw muck at him, make him wince and curse. In so many ways India is so much more fucked up than the US, even though the US is fucked up in its own ways. But for now, he longs to be there, amid its rhythms, chaos, and pace of change. Fuck this Silicon Valley bubble he is in. He longs to reconnect with other forms of life, with the many dormant and forgotten parts of his self. A year in India, he feels certain, will be far more transformative than anything he will likely do in the Bay Area. He will learn and grow, perhaps see afresh how deep our stories run. It may be as much of a life-changing experience as the year of his arrival in the US nearly sixteen years ago. It could even become the start of something new and beautiful. The time is just right. He is so looking forward to this next chapter of life.

§

Thirty-six hours to go. Ved is returning home from his last round of gift shopping for India. On 101 South into San Francisco, the traffic is moving well. The radio station classifies the music now playing as nouveau flamenco. He taps a finger on the steering wheel and glances at the vivid sunset, hillsides, the ocean. His mind is lucid and calm. What a marvel, he muses, that his mind should bestow such beauty upon things that do not care a hoot about him.

His apartment is almost empty. Most of their suitcases stand packed in a corner. All he has to do is a final bit of cleaning, make one last trip to the storage site, and have Sunil pick up his car. The living room looks so much larger without the furniture. Anita is on the floor, raising a storm. Her toys lie scattered about her. He has never seen her so hyperactive. Perhaps she too senses that a big journey lies ahead. She rushes up to show him her cooking kit: tiny pots and pans, a gas stove, a pressure cooker. Rashmi is about to scold her for the ruckus when he stops her with a hand gesture.

From his pocket he pulls out two fist-sized ducks made of soft plastic—tradeshow goodies he found under his car seat, Omnicon inscribed on their sides—and gives them to Anita. She watches with her big eyes as he fills up the kitchen sink for their swim. The first one floats well enough, but the second one promptly drowns. Clearly not much of a duck, but the giggle it provokes in Anita echoes loud and clear in the empty room.